GIGANTA

AN EPIC TALE

GIGANTA

R A COOK

HMA PUB

Publisher of Books, Stories & Cards

Dedicated to
Haakon, Marius, and Anders

With a special mention to
Stella Dillard

GIGANTA, An Epic Tale
RA Cook
Copyright © 2021
All Rights Reserved

No portion of this book may be reproduced or transmitted in any form or by any means, electronic or mechanical, including photocopying and recording, or by an information storage or retrieval system without written permission from the author.

Cover and interior design by Rebecca Cook
Illustrations by Rebecca Cook
Edited by Antoinette L. Botsford

Text set in Georgia

Library of Congress Cataloging-in-Publication Data
Rebecca Cook

GIGANTA, An Epic Tale
by RA Cook
1. Juvenile Fiction   2. Fantasy & Magic

ISBN: 979-8-9883778-2-5

Library of Congress Control Number:
2021920988

Published in the United States of America
HMA Publishing
PO Box 3054, Friday Harbor, WA 98250
www.hmapublishing.com

First Edition

Table of Contents

Preface

In 1959, Herdís Egilsdóttir, author of many children's books, wrote her first story about Sigga, a human girl, and her friend, the Giantess in the Mountains, a troll. A cave near the small boat harbor in Reykjanesbær, Iceland houses a large sculpture of the Giantess. Outside the cave a plaque tells her story.

On a five-day visit to Iceland in the fall of 2015, I encountered the Gigantess in the Mountains, her cave, and the placard narrating Herdís Egilsdóttir's story in the town of Reykjanesbær. Intrigued with the Giantess and charmed by Icelandic troll and elf lore, I was inspired to write my own story.

All of the names and places in *Giganta, An Epic Tale* are fictitious, except for Reykjavik. Iceland's stark volcanic landscape and harsh, rugged climate is, however, very real. The country's wild and free nature holds deep magic and one can imagine sharing a world with trolls and elves.

The troll and elf vocabulary used is inspired by Old Icelandic and Old Welsh.

1
Giganta Meets Gustaf

In the pre-dawn silence Giganta listened to the faint sound of water dripping down the walls. A late night storm had soaked the inside of her cave. Rushing along the coastline, winter winds had swirled around the crescent-shaped boat harbor, hitting the town and nicking the stone shelter that jutted into the frothy gray water. The fierce rain leaked through the gargantuan wooden door, and now a dank puddle of cold seawater pooled in front. "Brrr," she shivered. She would have to mop up before too long.

She lit the remnant of yesterday's candle and surveyed the chilly room. The fire in the immense stone fireplace that covered the back wall had long since died. Her eyes wandered past the rocky opening to the nearly empty kindling box. "How can I live here another day?" she whispered.

Arms raised over her head, she stretched. Draping a threadbare shawl around her shoulders she swung her long, boney legs over the edge of the bed. Giganta's bare feet touched the damp floor. "Brrr," she said again. Reaching under the bed, her hands skimmed the floor for her worn slippers. She grabbed one, then the other, and slid her feet into them; within minutes her toes felt warmer.

Stiff from a night of restless sleep, Giganta stretched again and scuffed over to the kindling box to build a fire with the last of the wood. Without turning around she reached backward with a long gangly arm for the matches, but the box wasn't there. Twisting her huge angular body right, then left, her eyes searched the dim room until they landed on the small wooden container. "Ah ha!" she grunted. "There they are, the wooden sticks that make fire." And then, in the tongue she had learned at a young age she said, "*Leiki. Matches.*" She repeated the word several times. "Matches. Matches," she said. "That's what the humans call them." She stood up, and in three long strides crossed the room. Snatching the matchstick box, Giganta struck a flame and bent down to light the fire. "There," she said, rubbing her hands together. "The room will be warm soon."

She knew the town folk would soon pound on her cave door with their morning offerings, so she slipped on her rumpled dress and tried to smooth down her scraggily long hair. Through the crack in the rocky ceiling, Giganta glimpsed the gray sky. Taught long ago to gauge the day's temperature by sight, she noted with conviction, "It's going to be a cold day." She threw on a heavier woolen shawl and walked over to the leaky door the mayor had the workers install a month ago. "I will tell him to fix the leaks," she said. Then Giganta, the town troll, yanked opened the door and walked out to greet the people.

✳

A placard near Giganta's cave tells her story. As the legend goes, Inga, an adventurous, young human girl first encountered Giganta on a trek into the mountains. Giganta told Inga that she had been wandering the hills looking for other trolls. During her search she had encountered several elves who explained to her that the other trolls had gone away. Fleeing from the encroaching human disturbance the trolls had not waited for Giganta but had migrated deeper into the most secret places within the glacial mountains. Feeling lonely and forlorn, Giganta was glad to meet Inga. Once they became friends, Inga had convinced Giganta to come down from the mountains and live near humans. "We are good, and you are lonely. Please come," Inga said.

And so Giganta followed Inga down the mountains to live in a small town nestled in a harbor near the great city of Reykjavik. Soon after arriving in the town, Giganta rushed into the icy water and saved a small fishing boat and its crew in a bad storm. To reward her bravery, the mayor offered Giganta the stone shelter as her home. Since then, many people have visited Giganta, and for a long time she was comfortable and content in her cave. Giganta enjoyed the children, who came from all over Iceland to see her, and because they often sensed her loneliness, the tiniest ones left her their most precious gift—that of a pacifier. Hundreds of them dangled on strings inside her cave.

But life grew more difficult for Giganta after Inga, her trusted human friend, married and moved away. Visitors were often rude and inconsiderate. Some left trash at her door; others would come into her cave when she was not there. A few had even stolen some of the pacifiers. "I want to leave," she told the mayor one morning. "I cannot live like this. I am a troll after all." Fierce and upset, her voice boomed past the mayor and his morning entourage, spewing anger into the harbor waters. A dark squall splattered rain on passersby.

Dismayed, the mayor knew most of the townspeople loved their resident troll, so to cajole Giganta he promised, "We'll patrol the area, Giganta. It won't happen again." But it happened again and again. Even though the mayor hired guards to protect Giganta's cave, they often fell asleep, hid behind her cave, or ignored their duty and drank too much before creeping away in the night. Some even accepted bribes to sneak travelers into her cave when she wasn't there. One day Giganta had enough and stomped out of her cave. The ground shook with her anger as she strode past the buildings and highway.

"Where will you go?" the mayor called to her as she was leaving.

"Into the mountains. I will find the other trolls," she said, waving her fist. "I want to be with *them* now."

So Giganta set off toward the mountains. She trudged over rough black lava-encrusted plains, surprising two sheep grazing in the sparse fields. Charcoal gray clouds dumped rain on Giganta and the wooly creatures. Coursing sideways, the water pelted her body and the moss-covered stones she tromped over. She didn't seem to mind when the wind whipped her straggly black hair into her eyes. She plodded onward until she reached the place where the rough black rock met the land's smooth dome-like mountains.

These were new mountains, born of great force, erupting from the ocean floor a millennium before the Vikings sailed to the tiny continent. Only the elves and trolls knew when the land had been formed. They remained the primordial guardians of the land and protected the secret places and sacred temples.

As Giganta approached the mountainous terrain, a shaft of light cut through the murky sky. She followed the sunbeam, climbing the first ridge and then proceeded to the top of a higher one, where a waterfall crashed over a craggy volcanic cliff. The rain stopped as she reached the precipice. Wondering where to go next, Giganta dried herself in the warm sun and rested for a spell. The waterfall's roar deafened her thoughts. Cold glacial water soothed and diminished the constant chatter inside her head—human chatter she'd grown used to when living among them. She'd have to let the humans go, she thought—and their language too. She sighed.

Sitting there, deliberating her next move, Giganta worried that she had forgotten much of the old language, the ancient tongues of trolls and elves, when without warning she felt something alight on her right shoulder. "What?" she said with a start.

"Hello!" rang a cheery voice.

Giganta turned to see a tiny elf with a scruffy beard standing on her shoulder. He flipped his tall pointed brown hat out of his eyes and in elf language asked, "Where ya goin'?"

"I saws you from way off and
wondered where you was goin'."

To Giganta's surprise she understood the strange sounds and replied in kind, "I don't know. Where do you think I should go? I'm looking for the trolls."

The elf jumped down from Giganta's shoulder onto a pock-marked volcanic boulder. Putting one hand on a hip and raising his other hand, he pointed his long, bony forefinger straight ahead. "Over there," he said with pride. "Way, way over there is where them trolls are."

Giganta scanned the mountainous terrain ahead. Rain-filled dark clouds glowered above the glacial fjords; steam vapors from geothermic fissures rose eerily from the near-by valleys. "Have you seen them?" she asked eagerly. "How many are there?"

"Hmm." The little elf rubbed his hairy chin and thought for a few moments. "Well, I don't rightly know today. Haven't been in troll country for quite some time." Then the elf brightened, his face lit up, and he said, "Maybe to-morrow I'll know. You never know what tomorrow will bring, do ya?"

"No. Certainly not," Giganta sighed. "I don't even know what today will bring." Giganta stared at the little man. "Who are you, anyway?" she said. "Where did you come from?"

"I been followin' you for a while," the elf said. "I saws you from way off and wondered where you was goin'." The elf smiled and jumped to another boulder. Looking down the waterfall he asked, "Where are *you* goin'?" Then the elf turned around to face Giganta. With his chubby little face sprinkled with spray from the waterfall he said, "Are ya hungry?"

"Why yes, I—I think I am," she said.

"Good!" His wide smile showed a few missing teeth. "Follow me." Then as quick as lightning, the elf shot up the next ridge. Amazed at the elf's speed Giganta loped after him. Once up the ridge she edged herself around a sharp bend, her giant feet barely finding space on the narrow trail. After twisting her huge frame around the diminishing section, she looked up to find the elf standing in the middle of the muddy path waiting for her. Some distance ahead of him a massive jumble of volcanic black rock had fallen across the path. "Come on!" he cried as he motioned to the lava formation. "Hurry up! The doorway will close soon."

"Doorway?" Giganta squinted, narrowing her vision. "I don't see a doorway."

"Come on! Just here. Come now!"

The elf's urgency piqued Giganta's natural curiosity, and she followed him until they arrived at the towering rockslide. Then the elf vanished—slipped out of sight right in front of her. Giganta couldn't imagine where he'd gone. "Where are you?" she called, spinning around. "What happened to you?"

"Psst. Over here," she heard him say. "Duck down; you'll fit."

"What?"

"Here. Over here," he said. "Just try it."

Crouching down, Giganta reached out with her right arm toward the elf's voice and, to her amazement, her hand disappeared. It seemed to have gone through an invisible wall. Testing the phenomenon a little further, she shoved more of her arm in and watched it disappear as well.

"Come on! Soup's ready," the elf said. "You can do it."

"Okay, but—but—where are we going?"

"Here. We're going here. You want to eat, don't you?"

"Yes, but—well, where is 'here'?"

"Right here. Now, come on!"

Giganta felt a little tug on her arm. Then she felt another, stronger tug. Taut with fear, she dug her heels in. "Wait a minute," she said.

"We don't have a minute! The door is closing fast. You don't want your arm to be stuck, do ya?" With a mighty yank the elf pulled Giganta through the opening.

✳

At first she could see very little in the dimly lit cave. Once her eyes adjusted, Giganta took in her surroundings. Lining smooth curved stone walls up and all the way across the ceiling were elaborate line drawings of strange looking animals and other unfamiliar beings. Each painting, finely rendered in natural, earth-colored pigments, dazzled and filled Giganta with wonderment. "What is this place?"

"Well, those people in the city might call it a church," the elf said.

"I thought we were going to eat. We can't eat in a church, can we?" Then Giganta mumbled under her breath in troll language, "Why I've never heard of such a thing, eating in a church. A troll would never go to a temple to eat. Never."

"Just follow me," the elf said in troll language. "You'll see." Then he whisked down the shadowy trail.

"Wait! You speak troll?" Giganta lurched after the elf. "Wait, I say! You haven't told me your name. What's your name?"

The little elf stopped, turned, and smiled. "Why my name is Gustaf, Head Scout for the Inner Earth elves," he said. Taking off his pointed hat, he bowed to Giganta as if she were royalty. Then he stood up, popped his hat back on and said, "Glad to make your acquaintance. And yes, I do speak troll. *All* elves do. Now come on! We're gonna miss the first course."

Encouraged by the thought of food, not to mention her continued curiosity, Giganta followed the elf around a hairpin corner. A few yards later Gustaf led her down a stone stairwell and into a dark, tapering tunnel. "Watch your head," the elf cautioned, pointing up to the cave ceiling. Bending down to accommodate the shortening height of the cave, Giganta crept along. The farther she went, the darker it got until she lost sight of the elf. Using her large feet to feel the way, she crept forward, planting one foot before the other. Spreading her arms to keep her balance, she touched the cool sides of the stone tunnel. It was then she wished she had a few matches such as the humans made. Just as the thought crossed her mind, Gustaf appeared, carrying a small, brightly lit torch.

"Use this," Gustaf said and thrust the flaming stick upward toward Giganta.

"Thank you," she said. Holding the tiny torch between her forefinger and thumb, Giganta walked, leaning down to adjust her body to the ever-decreasing passage. It relieved her to see more of the winding trail before them. But it wasn't long before the cave tunnel narrowed, and Giganta's shoulders rubbed against the walls. Worried, she asked, "How much farther?"

"Just ahead," Gustaf said and whistled to ease the troll's mind. So loud and bold was his whistle it echoed down the tunnel, bouncing off the walls until the passageway was bursting with sound.

Despite Gustaf's boisterous, merry tune Giganta continued to feel alarmed. The narrowing tunnel didn't help. "I'm feeling very squeezed here," she said, bending down even further. "Is the tunnel going to get any smaller? I'm not sure I'll fit if it does."

"Don't worry. We're almost there. Look." Gustaf pointed to a pinprick of light ahead.

"Oh!" Giganta gasped. "I see it!" In her excitement she tried to stand, cracking her head on the rocky ceiling. "Ouch!" she said, rubbing her head.

"Careful now, Miss Troll." Gustaf laughed. "Don'cha hurt yourself." Out of the blue, Gustaf handed her another torch. "Here, take this," he said. Tipping his head back, he sniffed the air. "Hmm, can you smell it? Lunch is being served." Gustaf's eyes widened with delight. "Let's go!" he said, and took off again.

With one torch in each hand, Giganta could see down the rocky corridor much better and moved forward confidently. As she hobbled along, the walls widened. Soon she could stand without grazing her head. "Ah, this is better," she sighed. Giganta caught a whiff of something delicious. "Now I smell food," she said.

The aroma of freshly baked bread pulled Giganta forward until the pinprick of light swelled; the walls opened wider and wider; the ceiling grew higher and taller until she entered a vast stone cathedral. Carved basalt columns braced the roof of the cave, soaring fifty feet in the air; the ground, swept clean of debris, was smooth under her feet. A thin shaft of light pierced the middle of the immense room. Giganta stopped. All around her was silence. She strained her ears to listen for something but all she heard was her stomach growling.

"Where are you, Gustaf?" she said. Her voice echoed throughout the chamber.

"Over here … I'm over here."

Waving the torches in front of her, Giganta found Gustaf perched on the edge of a large carved ledge. A natural spring seeped from the smooth rock wall nearest him and into an enormous carved stone chalice. Steam wafted from the sky blue water. "We need to wash before entering. It's the custom here," he said, pointing to the water. "Since we have been 'out there'," he gestured toward the tunnel, "we have to wash all the human energy off. Keeps us healthy," he said. "We don't want to infect the others."

"Oh. No. Surely not," Giganta agreed. She stuck the torches into a crevice and plunged her hands in the water. It felt soft, almost luxurious, and very warm. Giganta was sure she had never washed with this kind of water before. Her cave water had only felt cold and harsh.

"Hurry now, Miss Troll. I'm really hungry." Gustaf massaged his stomach. "I sure hope Sabina made those yummy cakes again. I love 'em."

"Anything would taste good right now," Giganta said, splashing her face. "Do they have troll food there, too?"

"Of course. Trolls will be at the feast today. It's a celebration! All trolls are invited."

"A feast? Why, uh, I didn't know we were going to a feast!" Giganta looked down at her shabby clothes, wondering if she was presentable. She had not thought about her appearance until now. Nervous, she brushed the dirt off her sleeves and tried to press the wrinkles out of her skirt. She had never been to a feast before. "Do I look all right?" she said.

Jumping down from the ledge, Gustaf eyed Giganta. With hands clasped behind his back he made a wide circle around the troll looking her up and down, inspecting her. "Yes," he said, nodding, "I think you'll do." Then he walked around the chalice, reached up on his tiptoes and slid an oblong, highly polished ebony stone from right to left. A gigantic archway began to open. Giganta stood in awe as she watched the heavy stone door slide back.

"I'll lead the way," Gustaf said. Goose-stepping as if he was head of a parade, he marched ahead of Giganta. "Today is the equinox," he announced. "We always have a grand celebration on the equinox. All the elves and trolls gather. It is an important day for us. You have come just in time for the beginning of spring."

2
The Elf Kingdom

Walking through the rough-hewn stone archway was like moving from the deepest part of night into a shining, bright morning. Green rolling hills and bountiful fields of colorful wildflowers stretched as far as Giganta could see. Birdsong blended with elfin laughter in the distance. Giganta saw groups of the little people frolicking, walking together toward what looked like a grand stage with towering red, orange, and blue flags whipping in the breeze. Music filled the air and the delectable scent of fresh-baked goods was unmistakable.

"What is this place?" she asked.

"Why it's the Elf Kingdom, my home and—where we're gonna eat!" Gustaf said. "I'll be goin' now. Just follow the road. Meetcha there!" Then turning and waving goodbye, Gustaf left without another word.

Lulled by the expansive pastoral landscape Giganta stood transfixed, wonder-struck as she watched Gustaf's tiny feet zoom down the road with breakneck speed. Yet she wasn't worried about being left behind this time.

From her troll height of three meters she could see the way to the equinox festivities. In her memory, Giganta couldn't recall ever seeing such a wondrous spectacle; the humans had nothing to compare with what fanned out before her. She felt giddy—almost lightheaded—filled with the infectious enthusiasm, joy and camaraderie surrounding her.

A loud grating noise jolted her out of her euphoric state. Swiveling her giant body she witnessed the great stone door slide and close shut. Within minutes there was no sign of the mysterious portal; the entrance was sealed. The outer world of humans was gone. An extraordinary sense of wonder made her forget how hungry she was. "The equinox," she said and then repeated the word in troll language. "Jofuvensol." Sounding out every letter, she repeated the word several times and then strode toward the celebration.

Taking long troll strides Giganta stretched her giant legs. She felt good moving at her normal troll pace again. Knowing there would be other trolls at the festival, she tried to recall a few from her past but no one came to mind. She knew many of the trolls had moved long ago to another dimension. That's how it happened she was left behind. The other trolls had warned her to stay away from humans but she had been too curious and sometimes sneaked down below the ridge line onto the steaming black lava fields to watch the humans who had encroached upon troll territory. Deeper and deeper the humans had invaded troll country. One after another, human families had built homes on sacred troll ground. The elf scouts alerted the trolls about the advancing humans but there were fewer and fewer safe places for them and so most of the trolls chose to slide through a dimensional barrier that few humans could penetrate. Giganta had not been ready for the change once she met Inga, her human friend. She had chosen to stay behind and live with the humans. Now she was determined to find the other trolls again. How many trolls were left? Would any of them remember her?

✳

Giganta lumbered along and covered a great distance at a quick pace because of her troll size. She headed toward the Elf Village and slowed when she came to a 'y' in the road. Here, the narrow country dirt road diverged and the right fork transformed into a wide, welcoming lane. Between the two roads a royal blue signpost lettered with gilt gold read *The Queen's Avenue.*

"Welcome to The Queen's Avenue."

Giganta jumped and swung around. "What?"

"Welcome, I said. Are you heading to Jofuvensol?"

Staring with fascination, Giganta realized the sign was talking. It had a mouth and moving lips. She laughed out loud. "Why, yes, I am," she said.

"Good! Go this way," the sign said. At that moment, a long, slender blue hand slid out of the end of the sign and pointed down The Queen's Avenue.

"Thank you," Giganta said, all the while marveling at the novelty of a talking sign. "You're a wonder!"

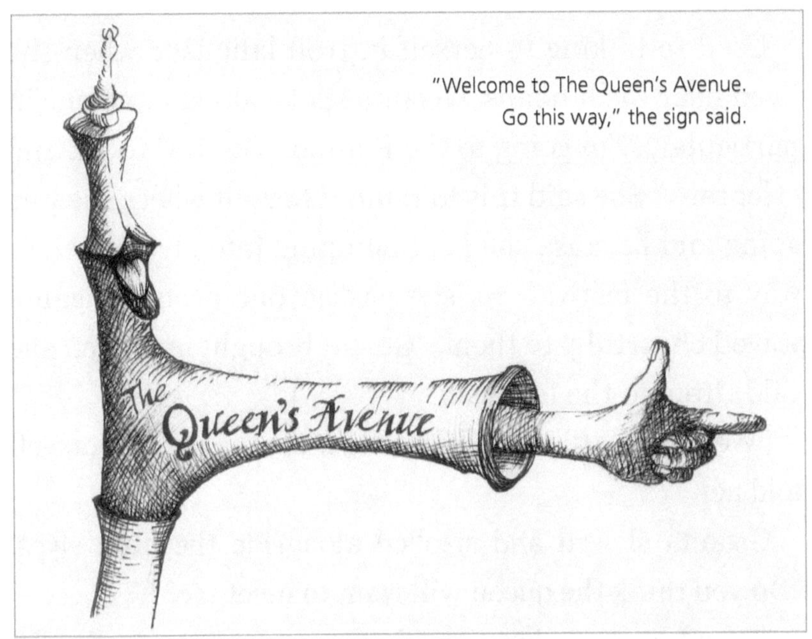

*

The instant her foot stepped onto The Queen's Avenue the road turned lime green. Startled, Giganta hesitated. She watched in astonishment as the fluorescent color gushed down the avenue toward the village center. As the bright hue spread, each side of the road came alive with flowers of orange calendula, deep purple lupine, and sky blue forget-me-nots—all in full bloom. Not far ahead Giganta saw quaint buildings lining both sides of The Queen's Avenue. Each had a gilded door with freshly washed stained glass windows. Every window had a lavish window box filled with basil, thyme, bergamot and other robust herbs. Most of the buildings boasted spirals with decorative banners; each banner proclaimed the start of spring. Flags emblazoned with the royal crest of the Queen of Elves flapped in the gentle breeze.

Used to talking to herself in troll language when she lived near the humans, Giganta spoke aloud to no one in particular, "I'm going to the Equinox Festival to eat and celebrate." She said this to remind herself where she was going and because she kept bumping into elves on their way to the festival. As she passed one group, Giganta waved cheerfully to them. "Gustaf brought me here," she said, "to join the festival."

"Well then, Milady, follow us to meet the queen," one elf told her.

Giganta slowed and strolled alongside the little elves. "Do you think the queen will want to meet me?"

"Of course," another elf said. "Our queen *loves* trolls. She welcomes all trolls into her kingdom."

Relieved, Giganta clapped her hands and said with glee, "I was hoping you'd say that, Mr. Elf. I haven't been here before, you know. The other trolls left me in the outer world long ago. I came here looking for them because I want to live with them again. That's how I met Gustaf."

"Well, at least one troll will be at the festival," another elf offered.

"Only one troll?" Giganta's face fell. "Are there any others?"

"Uh, well, I don't rightly know." Then he brightened. "Our wise Queen Drotti knows though," he said, nodding to the other elves.

Then all the elves nodded their heads together and said in unison, "Yes, ask the queen. She knows! Welcome to Jofuvensol!"

✳

Soon Giganta found herself at an enormous festival. When she entered the stage arena, she came to an elaborately carved wooden table laden with bounteous foodstuffs. Platters of bread, fruit and strange-looking squash ran down the length of the table; goblets of wine and cider awaited, billowing saucers of cream and butter rested near tempting baskets of pumpkin bread, poppy seed and sesame seed rolls, all glistening with egg-washed crusts. Everything looked delicious and smelled wonderful.

Towering over the lavish spread, Giganta reached for a large sesame seed roll. After smearing a swath of creamy butter on top, she took a big bite. "Yummy!" she said. The butter ran down her chin. Wiping her mouth with the back of her hand, Giganta noticed it had become quiet. To her dismay, the entire village population had stopped eating and was staring straight at her.

It was then that Gustaf came forward. Bowing to the crowd he said, "This is my new troll friend, Giganta. I found her in the outer world and brought her here."

Elves roared with delight and pounded their half-filled mugs on the long table. Merrily, they raised their mugs to toast Gustaf and Giganta. One elf lifted his mug and cheered, "Skoal!" Mugs clashed and everyone sloshed down the last of their ale. The crowd's rowdy chatter rose to a thundering rumble as they refilled their mugs and stuffed their chubby faces.

Moving to the edge of the crowd, Gustaf raised his arm and gestured to Giganta. "Come over here," he yelled over the din. "I want you to meet Sabina, my wife. She makes the best pastries in the kingdom."

Sidestepping the long table and the raucous village elves, Giganta walked over to the couple and knelt down between them. "Why, hello, Sabina. I'm Giganta. Gustaf told me about your baking skills. I can't wait to taste one of your cakes."

"Over there." Sabina grinned with pride and pointed to a dessert table piled high with frosted rolls, cakes and cookies. "Take a few. As you can see there is plenty!" At the end of the table there was also a fountain of melted chocolate. The heated, luscious-smelling chocolate flowed down over three tiers into a round moat. Around the moat large crystal bowls burgeoned with red ripe freshly picked strawberries. And nearby the fountain stood a troll. Giganta's eyes widened. Another troll! "That's Ilg," Sabina said, "our resident troll. Gustaf told him you were coming."

When Ilg heard Sabina's voice, he tried to hide behind the chocolate fountain, but he was too tall and round. Realizing they had seen him, Ilg kneeled behind the pastry table to get out of sight and toppled a three-tiered cake. Fumbling with embarrassment, Ilg tried to pat the cake back together, but his big troll hands flattened the layers like flapjacks. The frosting oozed out and dripped down into the heated chocolate. Both Sabina and Gustaf laughed at the mess he'd made. Ilg's face turned bright red. "Sorry," he whimpered.

"Don't be embarrassed, Ilg." Giganta walked over to him. "I'll help you. I'm Giganta. As you can see, I'm a troll too."

Giganta held out her hand palm up, in troll tradition, to greet Ilg.

Rising from the ground, Ilg licked his sticky fingers, and then clasped Giganta's hand. "Uh, hello. I'm Ilg. Welcome to the Elf Kingdom."

As she felt the warmth of Ilg's hand, Giganta knew she and Ilg would be friends for life. Finally, she thought, she was with her own kind! A sudden and unexplained feeling came over her and with a twinge in her heart, Giganta gave Ilg a big troll hug. She continued to hold on to him long after troll etiquette deemed polite. "I'm so glad to meet you, Ilg! Do you live here?"

Embarrassed for the second time in front of Giganta, Ilg's face turned bright red again. He looked down at his big bare feet for a long minute and toyed with the surrounding dirt. Then, so as not to look Giganta in the eye, he turned away and like a cyclone his words spewed out. "Well, I live just on the edge of the village near that cave over there." Ilg whirled around with great force and pointed to a wall of basalt stone. In a loud voice he continued, "When I came here, the queen granted me a cottage and asked me to keep the village grounds clean. I fix things that break. Yes, that's it! I fix things—and—and—and I take care of the field animals when they are sick, too."

Somewhat stunned by the force of Ilg's outburst, Giganta stood back a little. "Oh," she said. "You're a handyman."

Ilg tilted his head and scrunched up his face. "A what?"

"A handyman. That's what the humans call someone who cleans and fixes things."

"Oh." At a loss for words, Ilg looked down and shuffled his feet. He wasn't sure he liked being called something other than his true troll name. But he knew he liked Giganta. He felt as if he had been waiting for her for a long time.

∗

Just then trumpets rang out and music burst forth from the large orchestra that had gathered. A dozen white split-tailed birds circled and soared overhead as a loud murmur rose from the crowd. "The queen is arriving!" Gustaf said. He grabbed Sabina's hand, and they ran to greet Her Majesty's Royal Company.

Unsure of what to do next, Giganta stood near Ilg, who had not moved. Together they watched the royal procession enter.

At the head of a long trail of elves the queen, dressed in purple and green finery, tossed her long red braids back as she walked toward the stage. Her crown of jewels and wildflowers sparkled in the brilliant sunlight. On top of her golden staff a large green stone sparkled green and purple light onto the ground before her. The royal elves who followed the queen—male and female alike—strutted in stylish brocade suits, tailored with fine cloth, and embellished with pearls and sacred elf gems. Each carried a banner signifying their rank and status within the royal company.

Awestruck by all the regalia and pomp, Giganta marveled as the queen's procession passed before her. She had never seen anything like this. When the six trumpet blowers finished announcing the procession's entry, the queen glided toward the stage where, with the touch of her staff, three wide golden stairs appeared.

Resplendent, Queen Drotti of the Elves climbed the stairs and positioned herself on center stage. An immense royal banner behind her flapped in the breeze as the crowd hushed when she raised her arms in salute. "Welcome, dear ones," she said. "It is a glorious day for the equinox! Let us celebrate. Let us continue to eat, drink and be merry on this day and many more to come. Now we shall dance until dawn. Carry on!"

The giddy crowd roared and clapped and then the orchestra struck up a lighthearted reel. A few couples twirled on to the dance floor, and then more and more took on the frolic until the whole village was dancing. The men swung their partners around and around until the music changed. Everyone formed into long lines, each line facing another. When the women lifted their long skirts ankle high Giganta saw their tiny feet working very complicated and intriguing dance steps. Facing their partners, the men jigged around the women, then squatted and goose-stepped and then jigged around them again and again until everyone was breathless. A tremendous energy vibrated the ground so much the earth shook beneath their feet. Captivated by the dance, Giganta said, "Oh, my, I'm sure I could never dance that way."

Before she could say another word, Ilg grabbed Giganta and swirled her into the dance circle. "Let's dance!" he said and guided her into the middle of the bedlam. Together they danced with big, clumsy troll feet to the lively music, moving with the crowd faster and faster until Giganta's head was swimming. She threw back her long black hair and laughed. Her heart was light and, for the first time in a great long while, she felt happy.

After a few more rousing dances and exuberant spins Giganta pleaded to Ilg, "Stop! I need to catch my breath."

Ilg stopped on the dance floor. Squeezing Giganta's arm, he gave her a worried, perplexed look. "Have I done something wrong?"

"No, of course not. Don't worry. I'm just out of breath." Giganta gulped air. "I've come a long way today. Can we sit down? I want to know more about the other trolls. How can I find them?"

"Oh."

"Come on. Just for a little while," Giganta said. Taking his arm she dragged a reluctant Ilg away. Collapsing on a grassy knoll above the dance floor, Giganta took a few long breaths, then patted the ground: "Here. Sit here, Ilg."

Ilg crouched next to Giganta, his face red. He felt nervous and tongue-tied. Bashful, he didn't know what to say. Stuttering he said, "I—I ho—hope I—have—have not hurt you."

Before Giganta could utter a word, the ground shook violently underneath them. "Oh!" Giganta clutched the grass on either side of her. Seconds later the earth shook; it cracked and split a hand's width apart in front of them. "Oh, no!" Giganta threw her hands over her eyes in horror.

"An earthquake!" Ilg shouted. "It's the volcano! Run!" Ilg grabbed Giganta's hand and yanked her up. Together they ran toward the upland fields.

"What about the others?" Giganta shouted, but Ilg didn't answer. Instead, he pulled harder on her arm and ran faster.

3
A Dangerous Journey

Some time later Giganta awoke in the darkened womb of a cave. Even though she was groggy, Giganta remembered there had been a massive earthquake. At the cave entrance Ilg's big, hulking silhouette stood, looking out. "Ilg," she asked, "where are we?"

For a few moments Ilg stood motionless as if glued to the ground. Without turning, he replied, "Safe. We're safe." He stepped away from the cave opening and with a clear sense of dread trudged over to Giganta. Staring down at her, looking straight into her worried eyes he added, "But we must find the others. They ran too." Extending a strong hand Ilg said, "Come. We must go."

"Where are the others?" Giganta brushed herself off. "How will we find them?"

"Follow me," Ilg said and took off down the rocky slope at a fast pace.

"Where? Where are they?" Giganta called out but Ilg didn't answer. Swinging back her long hair with fierce determination, she followed Ilg, for she too, wanted to find the

Without turning, Ilg replied, "Safe. We're safe."

village elves. Ilg was quick and agile for a troll. His shy, un-
assuming behavior and fumbling at the dessert table had
long since disappeared. Stumbling over a maze of newly

fallen lava rocks Giganta yelled, "Wait!" But Ilg did not look back or slow down.

Without a moment's hesitation, intending to skirt the elves' village, Ilg headed toward the green rolling hills now blocked by a massive rockslide. Above the crumbled black lava stood an enormous basalt column ridge. The tall, symmetrically shaped columns, formed by the recent volatile earth shift, stood well over 20 meters high. Hand over hand, foot over foot, Ilg climbed one steep cubic column and over to another. On and on he went. Even with her big troll body the terrain was difficult for Giganta, but she did her best to follow Ilg. Up, up, up they went. Several times Ilg looked back to make sure Giganta was still behind him, but he didn't stop. Finally, reaching the top, he waited for Giganta. Just as she arrived near the summit, Ilg reached for Giganta and pulled her to level ground.

"Whew," Giganta said, wiping her forehead with the back of her hand. "Thank you, Ilg. That was a rough climb for me. I'm not used to it."

Ilg nodded and without a word took her hand. Together they walked across to the far side of the plateau. At the edge, a waterfall plummeted into a sequestered canyon. They halted at the precipice and Ilg peered into the vast opening. Sensing the need for silence, Giganta watched uncertainly as Ilg stared into the deep gorge.

Squinting, hardly breathing, Ilg searched the canyon landscape. At last he said, "There. There they are!" Breaking into a smile, he pointed to a small, dark cave opening on the other side of the gorge where a few of the village elves had gathered. Ilg cupped his hands and made a howling sound that echoed throughout the canyon. Giganta could just barely see the tiny elves. Their cheering voices bounced against the ancient volcanic walls and floated up to the top of the canyon.

Cupping one hand around his ear to hear the elves' reply, Ilg grinned. With a big sigh of relief he said, "They tell me everyone made it." Then all at once he bounded with great force across the stream. "Follow me," he said and waved to Giganta as he leaped onto a few pock-marked lava boulders that edged the waterfall. Landing hard on the other side, his huge frame quivered from exertion. Giganta saw him hesitate. She was tired too. The day had been long. Yet she knew nothing would stop Ilg from continuing the journey. Ilg gestured toward a narrow, rocky trail. "Here's the way. Follow this trail," he said. Then shaking off his weariness, Ilg sprinted down the path, once again leaving Giganta to fend for herself.

With mixed emotions Giganta sighed at the prospect of facing another unfamiliar trail alone. Though relieved the elves were safe, she dreaded the steep pathway ahead. The long rocky path strewn with sharp volcanic pebbles made walking difficult. The pitted, irregular footpath, carved into what had been molten lava eons ago, was riddled with switchbacks. Her knees buckled several times when she rounded the last few hairpin corners. When Giganta saw Ilg waiting at the bottom of the canyon for her, she breathed easier.

Shy, Ilg took Giganta's hand and smiled. "It's not far now," he said, squeezing her fingers. Together they walked to the trail's end near the waterfall where a thunderous, cold downpour fed into a deep, crystal clear pool. About an acre in size, the pool poured into a gushing river that extended as far as the eye could see. By now all the village elves had gathered. They stood on the other side of the pool near the river and cheered when they saw Ilg and Giganta coming toward them. Ilg leaped onto a lava boulder and then another and another until he crossed the pool. When he got to the other side, the village elves assembled around him, everyone talking at once. In the uproar no one noticed Giganta, who feeling shy and estranged, was still waiting across the water. In the middle of the loud happy bustle Ilg looked back, remembering Giganta. "Come," he said and motioned to her, "join us."

Brightening, Giganta mimicked Ilg's crossing. Surprising herself, she deftly jumped on one boulder and then another until she landed with relative ease on the other side. Gustaf and Sabina met her at the water's edge. "We're so happy to see you again," Gustaf said.

Sabina reached up and touched Giganta's arm. "Yes," she said. "Very glad to see you!"

"Is everyone all right?" Giganta said.

"Of course," Gustaf said. A frown crossed his face as he cocked his head to the side and whispered, "But we don't know if *Musterihof*—the Great Temple—is damaged."

"Musterihof? The Great Temple? Where is that?"

"A ways from here," Gustaf said, "I can take you there but first you must go see Queen Drotti. She awaits."

With Gustaf on one side and Sabina on the other, the elves escorted Giganta to where the waterfall splashed and thundered into the pool. The three of them walked around the roaring water until they were on the other side looking out through the downpour. Ice-cold spray washed their faces and dampened their clothing. Because of her height, Giganta had to lean down as they entered the hidden cave; but once inside, the high carved ceiling allowed her to stand upright, enabling her to take in the extraordinary cave. Although the water had been deafening, inside the cave was quiet as an underground vault. From every angle, bright green moss insulated the walls, ceiling and ground, covering the entire room, top to bottom. Dappled lighting accented the mossy carpet, showcasing random dabs of orange, yellow, and red blooming wildflowers. Ahead, a brilliant shaft of light poured down upon the queen and her court.

"Your Majesty," Gustaf said, bowing. "I've brought you Giganta. As you know she has been in the human world for a long time and knows them well. I believe she can help us."

Queen Drotti sat motionless for a moment and then nodded to Gustaf. "Thank you, Gustaf. You have done a brave and wondrous deed. I shall reward you." The queen stamped the end of her crystal staff and waved it toward Gustaf. At once his shabby clothing changed into an exquisitely tailored suit of clothing. His jacket, once a dirty khaki brown, transformed into a pale, foam-green satin brocade, each sleeve embroidered with deep green silk leaves and set ablaze with stitched Icelandic wildflowers. Around his neck hung a thick chain of gold; dangling from it was a shiny round gold medallion engraved with the royal household crest.

"Ah!" The entire queen's court gasped as they gazed at Gustaf's new finery. The crowd stood back and bowed in reverence, for this was a rare occasion. It was known throughout the elf kingdom that Queen Drotti rarely gave such splendid rewards.

"This is an honor, Your Majesty," Gustaf said, stumbling with words. "I ... I ..." was all he could muster.

"It is due," the queen replied and then turned her attention toward Giganta. "Now," she said, "let us discuss your journey, Giganta."

"Journey?" Giganta glanced around for Gustaf but he and Sabina had wandered over to another side of the cavern. Sabina was touching and admiring Gustaf's new embroidered sleeves. They were lost in their own whispers.

"Yes," the queen said. "You must go to Musterihof. We believe there has been damage. Your knowledge of humans, would be most helpful. Can you take your leave?"

"Why, yes, of course. I mean, I ... I guess I can try, Your Majesty. But how can I help and where—where IS—Musterihof? I don't know how to get there."

"Gustaf and Ilg will accompany you. It is imperative you go on this day. The Great Temple is in grave danger after the earthquake, I fear. Your journey will be long. We will dine first and then you must go."

Queen Drotti raised her staff and waved it further into the cave. The staff's crystalline light fell on a large alcove just beyond the queen and her court. Along one side of the room was a long table piled with food and drink. Next to the alcove was a steaming deep blue, morning glory pool about three meters in diameter. Its soft, wavering blue light showed the beginning of a path that wound around the pool and led into a large, dark lava tunnel. "It is there you will go," the queen said as she raised her staff, "but first, join us. We have set a table for you."

Precisely at that moment, Giganta felt Ilg come from behind and take her elbow. Together they followed the queen and her court to the table. "Please sit here next to me," the queen said, motioning to a chair that was big enough for a troll. Ilg escorted Giganta to the table and then stood behind her. "Ah," sighed Queen Drotti as she eased into her makeshift throne. "It is always good to eat before a long journey. Don't you agree?"

"Yes." Giganta grabbed a clump of juicy red grapes. Hungry, she tossed a few in her mouth and then reached for the cheese and bread. After gobbling down a few bites she said, "This is delicious. I *am* hungry. Thank you."

"You are most welcome. Please. Have as much as you want. Fortify yourself, for the trip will be long." Queen Drotti urged and sipped from a crystal goblet. "My chef has packed food for you and the others. Ilg will carry it. I must warn you that you will find that some of the trip will be difficult. You will need the food and Ilg and Gustaf's help."

"I see. What must I do once I get to Musterihof?"

"You will know when the time comes," the queen said, "and there will be plenty of time along the way. But make haste, you must start the journey *now*," she commanded and then clapped her hands.

Gustaf, who had been wolfing down his meal, perked up his ears at the queen's signal. Wiping his mouth, he puffed out his chest, snapped his heels to attention. "Your Majesty, we are ready."

Ilg gulped down the rest of his food and took the provisions from the chef. "Your Majesty, I too, am ready," he said.

"Then you must go," the queen said. "We will wait for your return. Safe journey, my friends."

Giganta bowed. With a reverent nod from Queen Drotti and wave of her staff, Giganta followed Gustaf. Ilg took up the rear, shouldering their supplies. In single file they walked solemnly around the cerulean blue pool and into the darkened lava tunnel.

4
Journey Into the Earth

"Ow! I can't see," Giganta said, bumping into a tapering stalactite column. Rubbing her forehead she demanded, "Gustaf! Where is the light?"

"Here. Here, Milady," Ilg said. He plucked the torch from Gustaf's hand and raised the light above his head so they could all see deep into the tunnel. The tunnel, shaped like an elliptical tube, was littered top and bottom with stalactites and stalagmites. An endless obstacle course awaited them. Ilg shuffled up to Giganta, looked into her eyes and warned, "Be careful. There are many of these solid drips down here. They are very hard and the ground is slippery. Don't worry though, your eyes will get accustomed to the dark. Soon you'll see better."

"Solid drips?"

"Yes. Look up," Ilg said and cast the torchlight toward the ceiling.

Stretching her neck, Giganta looked upward and then glanced to the nearest stalactite—the one she had collided with. In the shadowy light its massive form extended to the top of the tunnel, some seven meters high. She reached out to touch the tip. "It is slippery," she said.

"Yes," Ilg said and knocked on the stalactite nearest him. "They come up from the bottom too. See." Ilg waved the torch along the ground ahead. Hundreds of calcified forms rose from the tunnel's floor in mysterious formations, many of their stalactite counterparts touched each other with their moist, salty tips.

Even in the dim light, Gustaf's face turned bright red. "Oh, very sorry, Milady, I forgot to mention it," he said. "There are many of them things here." Chagrined, he turned to lead the way and with authority ordered Ilg. "Follow Giganta and stay close, mind you. There are steep stairs coming up."

Ilg, the tallest and strongest of the adventuring trio, took the rear position and held the torch high as they wove around the countless calcified obstacles. Down they went through the steep tunnel until they reached a set of very narrow, steep stairs. This time, remembering to caution Giganta, Gustaf said, "Now be careful here, Miss Troll. Them stairs are tricky."

Mindful of Gustaf's words, Giganta hugged the rock wall; careful to navigate the ancient stone stairs, which were shallow and not made for troll-sized feet. After climbing down a dozen steps, Giganta stopped and peered tentatively into the gloom, trying to get her bearings. From her vantage all she could make out was the coarse lava wall on one side of the stairs and a mysterious, black void on the other. When a loose rock rolled out from under her foot nearly tripping her, she grabbed a thick notch in the rough-hewn wall. Fearful of losing her footing, Giganta gripped the large protruding stone to steady herself and strained to hear the sound as the rock landed. But there was no sound. It was a long, long way down. "Ilg? Where is your light?"

From behind she saw the soft glow of Ilg's torch and heard his calming words: "Don't worry," he said. "I am right here with you. I won't let you fall."

Giganta tried to smile, but did not turn around. "Good," she said and continued down the stone stairs. "I trust you, Ilg." Her voice quivered. "Thank you."

Ten meters or so ahead, Gustaf, accustomed to the treacherous stairwell, continued to deftly march downward.

When a loose rock rolled out from under her foot nearly tripping her, Giganta grabbed a thick notch in the rough-hewn wall.

He stopped when he did not hear the trolls behind him, turned and signaled to them with a slow, melodic whistle. The encouraging sound filled the staircase, reverberating along the lava walls up to Giganta and Ilg and down into the darkened swell. Ilg smiled and joined in. Within a few minutes Giganta felt armored and soothed by the uplifting tune. Her fear diminished. "I have good friends with me now," she thought. "I am not alone. I will not be afraid," she whispered to herself often until Gustav's voice interrupted her chant.

"You are so right, Miss Troll. Ilg and I are here and you are here and together we are going to Musterihof." Out of thin air came another tiny torch, and Gustaf held the sparkling light above his head, enabling them to see down the passage. Gustaf looked over his shoulder at the trolls following him. "And besides," he said, "we're near a good place for us to rest." Then as an afterthought and with a big grin he continued, "I'm getting hungry. Aren't you?"

"Come to think of it, yes! I am hungry," Ilg piped in. "The hot cross buns I'm carrying smell good and I can't wait to chomp on 'em." Ilg chortled as he hefted the food pack further up on his shoulders, readjusting the weight.

Silent and still a bit shaken, Giganta concentrated on walking. Willing herself to continue, she focused on taking one step and then another and another while sliding her fingers along the stone wall for support. "I—I—uh, I don't know where I am but I know I'll be glad to get off these stairs!" she said.

When they reached the bottom of their downward spiral, they found an alcove off to the side of the stairs. In the stone niche were several large boulders situated around an elevated, flat ledge, reminiscent of a small table setting. "Put the food there," Gustaf instructed, motioning to Ilg. "Giganta, will you unwrap the treats? I'm starving!"

After Giganta pulled out the buns, cheese, and drink, Ilg and Gustaf grinned and each took a hearty bite. "Yum!" Gustaf said, licking his lips. "I know Sabina made these buns. She's the best baker in the village."

Weary, Giganta sat on one boulder and toyed with the wrapping on her portion. So far, the journey had been difficult and frightening. *What was it all for?* Why had she left her safe cave and her human friend, Inga, for this? Befuddled, she turned her gaze to the black hollow space across from them and asked, "How long will it be until we get to Musterihof?" Gustaf held up his hand, put a finger to his right temple and chewed, looking thoughtful. "Not long, I s'pose," he said, swallowing his food. "Let's see: we have to reach the Tarvessa—um, the Ice Palace first and—and then go over Brulock, the Great Lava Bridge—and, and into another tunnel before we reach Musterihof." He paused and then said, "Uh, another day I 'spect."

"*Another day?* Tarvessa? Brulock?" Giganta said, holding back tears. "Just how far *is it* to the Great—er, Musterihof?"

"Far," Gustaf said, rolling his eyes.

"*What?*" Giganta pounded her fist on the stone table. "What do you mean? I don't know if I can stand this one more day. I don't even know where I am or what I'm supposed to do when—or I should say—*if* we get to Musterihof!" Giganta's eyes teared. "What AM I supposed to do, Gustaf?" she asked.

"Now, now, Miss Troll. It will be all right. I promise," Gustaf said, patting the troll's hand.

"Yes, Giganta. Keep the faith," Ilg said. "It's not that far. Not far, not really far, I mean." Ilg turned to Gustaf for support. "Is it, Gustaf? It's not really far. No, not *really*—far, that is." Ilg fumbled with the food pack and pulled out a small flask of liquid. "Here, have some of this. It will fortify you," he said, shoving the bottle toward Giganta.

Without questioning its contents, Giganta took a deep gulp from the flask and then another one. Ilg and Gustaf watched in amazement as her eyes grew big as millstones. "What is this fiery stuff?" she asked, and took another swallow.

"Oh, well—uh, it's rugmol—that's what we call it. We make it from a grain that grows here," Gustaf said. "We always bring this special drink for medicinal purposes."

"Yes, Milady," said Ilg. "Mind yourself though, a little rugmol goes a long way," Ilg said. "Too much and ya get a smashing head."

"Shh," Gustaf said and cocked his head. "Hear that?"

"What? What is it?" Alarmed, Ilg shot up, ramrod straight, twirled around, then hunched his back, ready to attack.

Giganta, finishing yet another drought of the drink, slammed down the bottle and hiccuped. "I don't hear anything," she said.

Gustaf held a forefinger to his lips and motioned for the others to keep quiet. From deep within the chasm came the faint yet distinct sound of a mechanical engine. Gustaf cocked his head again; his little body taut, struggling to hear. "They're drilling again!" he shouted. "Hear that?" Furious, Gustaf stomped his feet and shook his head so that his shaggy beard swished back and forth like a wild horse's mane. "It's the humans! They're drilling! We have to leave now! Ilg, pack our things. Go this way!" Then Gustaf took off without another word.

"Wait!" Giganta called after him but Gustaf had already disappeared into a nearby corridor. Ilg corked the half-empty bottle of rugmol, stuffed his knapsack with the remnants of their lunch, and rushed after Gustaf.

Dizzy from too much rugmol, Giganta stumbled, trying to catch up, but Gustaf and Ilg were already far ahead. She wanted to race after them, but in her woozy condition her giant troll feet seemed separate from the rest of her body. Nonetheless, she struggled to catch up.

Ahead, Gustaf stopped when he came to a fork in the underground route. Pausing, he shoved a torch into a crack in the rock wall. Cupping his hands, he yelled, "Come on! Hurry! We have go to Tarvessa. Follow the light."

Through her bewildered fog Giganta heard Gustaf's voice, plain as day, echoing to her. She couldn't remember what "Tarvessa" meant. "Oh, my," she said and staggered down the long passageway. "I'm coming!" she yelled into the murky void. The further she went, the colder it got. Shivering, she untied the woolen shawl from her waist. She wrapped it tight around her shoulders, at once feeling its warmth and relieved she'd brought it from the old cave home. *How long ago had that been?* So much had happened that it seemed like eons ago. Never mind, she thought, pushing those thoughts away. Giganta snatched the torch Gustaf left, made the sharp turn and lurched down the pathway, wondering why the humans were drilling. *What were they up to now?*

✳

At the end of a 40-meter long corridor Giganta found Ilg and Gustaf waiting by a rocky, deserted shoreline. Her body tightened from the frigid air as she plodded toward them. The rugmol's medicinal effect was wearing off and she had a terrible headache. Yet despite her pounding head and queasy stomach, Giganta felt spellbound, awed by the spectacle in front of her. Across a shallow icy pond, stood Tarvessa, the Ice Palace. Over a kilometer high, soaring like a mountain, the palace was breathtaking. The massive frozen waterfall glistened in every shade of luminous blue. As if by magic, the water cascaded in long, phosphorescent ice ripples, smoothed over a millennium. A mysterious incandescent light glowed from within the satin sheen.

"Behold," Gustaf said, bowing. "*Tarvessa!* We must wait for permission to pass. Giganta can you hear it?"

"Oh, yes!" Giganta gasped. "It's alive. I hear it."

Gustaf nodded. "Tarvessa speaks only to those who can hear."

"Milady, what does it say?" Ilg asked.

For a long moment, Giganta stood motionless. Then she turned and walked around to the edge of the frozen, cerulean blue water and stared up toward the Ice Palace precipice. "Musterihof needs us," she said. "We must go soon. That is all."

"Right," Gustaf said and clicked his heels together. "This is the way to *Brulock*—The Great Lava Bridge—which we must cross. Our journey becomes very dangerous now so look alive!"

"I will stay behind you, Giganta, from now on," Ilg assured. "You will be safe. Don't worry."

Giganta nodded to Ilg and smiled. "Thank you, Ilg," she said and fell in line behind Gustaf. The small band moved around the magnificent waterfall palace and through another darkened hallway. After a hundred steps, the walls turned from black lava into layers of heavy frost, then ice—solid blue ice. Gradually the walls curved and before long resembled a large, rolling ocean wave frozen in time. "Brrr," Giganta said, rubbing her shoulders. "It is cold in here, too."

"Not to worry," Gustaf said. "We will be very warm, very soon."

Giganta hugged her shoulders and tried not to mind the cold. Relieved to be with Gustaf and Ilg, she escaped into her own thoughts.

As they moved through the ice tunnel, Giganta's gait slowed. An uncomfortable foreboding stirred within her as she mulled over what the voice inside the Ice Palace had told her—especially the one thing she had not told the others, deciding at the last second to keep it to herself. She hadn't intended to keep that part a secret, but there was no need to frighten them even though she was more afraid now than she had been while descending the stairs.

5
Brulock,
The Great Lava Bridge

As they neared the end of the ice tunnel, Giganta heard a distinct roar. The temperature was rising too. Ice, melting from the warmer outer air, seeped down in cold droplets on Giganta's head, wetting her dark tresses and trickling down her back. She shrugged off her shawl and wrapped it around her waist. "What's that sound?" she asked, cinching it.

"That?" Gustaf said and turned to face the trolls. Walking backwards, he yelled over the roar. "Oh, that's the sound of the lava river flowing down to the ocean." Gustaf waited for the trolls as they sloshed through the glacial puddles. A few steps away from them he said with a mischievous smile, "Hear that hiss? That means we'll soon be coming to *Brulock*, the Great Lava Bridge!"

Giganta felt fear ripple down her spine. Ilg stepped next to her. "Yes, Milady, we're nearing the bridge. Do not worry. You are safe with me and Gustaf. I promise."

"Quite right. Very," Gustaf said. "But there is only *one* safe way. Follow me and please, step alive!"

The hissing sound of Brulock grew louder once the trio broke out of the darkened tunnel. Soon they approached a heavily pitted lava plateau about an acre in size. They followed the narrow, winding trail that led across the rough terrain to the edge of the cliff. The tumultuous Icelandic sea lay below them. Mighty waves crashed against the steep rocky cliffs. A furious wind whipped Giganta's hair. Gustaf grabbed his hat when a sudden gust seized it. Shouldering their heavy pack, Ilg hunched against the gale and tightened his grip on their supplies.

Against a backdrop of golden light, they hiked in single file along the uneven cliffs with Gustaf marching in front, Giganta, in the middle, and Ilg close behind. The hard coarse lava cut into their feet as they picked their way along the coastal cliffs. Volcanic steam vents sent long wisps of sulfuric fumes into the chaotic air, causing them to wheeze and cough. Up ahead, Giganta spotted a stream of red, molten lava oozing into the water. As the scalding substance glugged into the sea, dark poisonous vapors billowed high into the diminishing light.

Without warning, Gustaf stopped and threw out his arms. His eyes grew big. "See that steam?" he said. "Take heed, now. That there haze is death. We can't breathe it." He waved his hands and warned, "It's comin' straight at us. We're gonna have to go around and approach Brulock from that side." Gustaf pointed across a deep ravine. "Follow me," he said and scurried down into the gully. Scrambling to the top of the adjacent ridge, he waved. "Over here! Hurry!"

Without hesitation or thought of consequence, Ilg and Giganta jumped into the ravine and followed Gustaf's footsteps up the ridge. Their huge troll feet made short work of the climb and it wasn't long before they caught up with the elf. "I thought you said there was only one way?" Giganta said, puffing from exertion.

"'Tis right," Gustaf answered. "I know the way—and a shortcut, too." He winked and gave Giganta an impish grin. "That's why I'm Head Scout for the Inner Earth Elves. Only *I* knows the shortcuts and secret trails. Come now. Let's waste no time!"

Just as they started out, the wind shifted again, sending the voluminous, deadly haze toward them. "Quick! Over there!" Gustaf motioned to a jagged lava formation jutting high above the trolls' heads. From a distance the towering outcrop resembled a prehistoric dinosaur lost between millennia. In less than a minute, Gustaf dashed around it, then poked his head back to check on the trolls' progress. His tall, pointy hat flopped over one eye as he waved to them. "This way! Hurry!" he yelled.

Sensing the impending danger, Giganta and Ilg caught up with Gustaf and without uttering a word, the trio rushed toward a mammoth jumble of fallen basalt columns. Once there, Gustaf leaned against the remains of an angular gray column and sighed with relief. "Whew," he said. "We made it past the smoke, but we're not safe yet. Come this way. We can rest once we get to the sand."

On the back side of the basalt ruins was a short, squatty lava tunnel. "Follow me," Gustaf said. He sprinted into and out of the other side of the tube in a few minutes. But because of their height, both trolls had to sit on their haunches and almost crawl through. Once Giganta squeezed out of the tunnel and rose to her full height, she beheld a long, black sand beach. Her eyes grew wide with delight at the sparkling black sand that stretched over a kilometer long. She stood for a moment, transfixed by the coal-black sand and raucous waves smashing against the rugged coastline.

Gustaf held up a hand; inhaling, he said, "Ah, take a big sniff of that breeze for it will be the last we'll smell the sea for quite some time."

"What do you mean, Gustaf?" Giganta stuck her toes into the black sand and burrowed them down until the warm sand covered her feet.

"Over there." Gustaf pointed. "See that smoke? That's the volcano! The Great Temple is near there and that is where we must go."

Giganta took several deep breaths.

"Don't worry, Giganta," Ilg said. "It won't be too hard and I'll keep you safe."

"Yes, Miss Troll, worry not. Remember, I know the way!" Gustaf said.

✳

Fortified by the fresh sea air, the small company walked down the shoreline in silence. The cold ocean soothed their sore feet and the salty breeze brushed their bodies, wiping their souls clean. Before long, Giganta felt hungry again. "Can we eat? My head is aching, and my stomach growls."

"Later," Gustaf said. "Methinks before nightfall we must cross the Great Lava Bridge."

"But you said—"

"Terribly sorry, Miss Troll, but methinks the wind will change soon. We must cross the bridge before—before—well, it is dangerous, Miss."

"How much farther?" Giganta asked.

"Look ahead," Gustaf said and extended his arm in the direction of a large formation of volcanic stones stacked haphazardly one on top of another, the shape reminiscent of a pyramid. "There," he said.

Just then they heard a loud roar. Giganta jumped back. "What's that?"

"*Eldsplodenryg!* The Great Volcano! It pours steadily now," Gustaf said. "Stay close behind me and step where I step." Turning, he headed toward the stone monument. As they approached the dark shrine, the landscape around the small party transformed as if they had stepped across an invisible line. Ahead of them, the ground was an endless stretch of dense charcoal black. There was no vegetation in sight—not even a blade of green grass. Beneath their feet, the thick rippled lava crust, solidified centuries ago, made walking difficult.

Giganta giggled. Even though she knew they were at risk, she couldn't help herself. The hardened, undulating magma reminded her of rich, dark frosting. "Look, Ilg," she said, pointing down, "chocolate cake frosting!"

"Yes, Milady." Ilg's tone was tinged with dread, for he knew better than Giganta what lay ahead.

*

In single file they crept over the ancient, rough surface, edging around the stone pyramid and down a barely visible trail. Volcanic steam vents littered the ground. The air smelled like rotten eggs. Breathing was hard. Giganta willed herself forward, concentrating on putting one foot ahead of another and focused her eyes on Gustaf's every move. Soon they came to the edge of another steep cliff. Below, steam billowed from molten lava as it oozed and swirled, the air crackling with heat. The ground under their feet trembled.

"Behold," Gustaf said. "*Heilaga Hraunvaten*, The Great Lava Lake. We must take the trail along this side of the lake to reach Brulock, the Great Lava Bridge, where we will cross."

"Gustaf, stop!" Giganta said, wiping her brow with the back of her hand. "You mentioned nothing about a lava lake." She loosened her shawl around her waist and leaned over the cliff. Despite the heat Giganta was momentarily transfixed as she stared into the steaming, molten lake. For a moment she was sure she saw a face in the middle of the red-hot lava. "The lake—I saw something."

"Do not look into that face you see in the lake," Gustaf warned. "The fire and steam will reach up and grab you if you stare too long. Then you are lost. It has happened before."

Giganta gulped and took a step backward.

"Milady," Ilg said, "What Gustaf said is true. I have seen it."

Giganta shivered. "I—I don't know if I can go on now. I'm—I'm too afraid."

"Now, now, Miss Troll," Gustaf said. Reaching up, he patted her hand. "We are here with you and know the way. You will be safe. Stay close and nothing will harm you, I promise. Now, come." Gustaf turned and walked along the cliff's edge, whistling a cheery tune. Squeezing her shoulder, Ilg nudged Giganta. With no other choice, she swallowed her fear and followed Gustaf. The heat baked their bodies as they trudged along the edge of Heilaga Hraunvaten. Sweat rolled down their faces. When they took in the coarse air, they coughed it back out. Ahead loomed the Great Lava Bridge, half hidden by volcanic steam.

Gustaf took off his sweat-drenched hat and bowed. "Behold, Brulock," he said. Torrid, eerie steam rose from either side of the bridge. The volcanic vapors were so opaque that the bridge appeared to be suspended over the lake, floating in a cloud of scalding mist. "The elders built this bridge as a gift to our queen before they left," Gustaf said. "It is revered by all in the Elf Kingdom."

At least a kilometer in length, the Great Lava Bridge was a mastery of stone masonry. Constructed of pumice rock and lime mortar, the massive ramp had been built to be sturdy, yet lightweight and flexible. To avoid the never-ending flow of escaping magma, the bridge arched high up and over the searing lake.

As the heat rose from the fiery depths, it singed Gustaf's beard, but he made no note of it. "Come. Step lively for we must cross quickly." He held up one finger and cautioned. "One at a time."

"Have, have you crossed before?" Giganta asked.

"I have crossed twice and returned twice before," Gustaf said.

"I have crossed once before," Ilg offered. "It is dangerous but you will make it. I will go first. Once I am on the other side, I will signal you to follow." Then, Ilg set off over the bridge. His huge body soon disappeared into the gloomy air. Giganta placed her feet on the ramp waiting her turn. She stared in vain to catch a glimpse of Ilg in the swirling vapors.

Halfway over, at the top of the arch, Ilg halted. "The bridge! It is broken," he yelled back. "It is weak!"

The quake that had shocked and reverberated throughout the Elf Kingdom a few days before had also wreaked havoc with Brulock. Wedges of bridge mortar had cracked and part of the pumice rock had given way so that a wide gap separated the two sides of the bridge.

Halfway over, at the top of the arch, Ilg halted. "The bridge! It is broken," he yelled back. "It is weak!"

"Jump across!" Gustaf hollered into the mist. "The bridge will hold!"

Stepping back a few meters, Ilg took a running start and leaped over the fissure. Just as he landed on the other side, his left foot slipped on a piece of cracked mortar and he fell to his knees. He roared as he slid backward. Grabbing onto the side of the ramp, he stopped short of going over. Left with one leg dangling over the side, he couldn't pull himself up to safety.

Ilg!" Giganta yelled. Turning to Gustaf she cried, "Help him. Please, Gustaf!"

Gustaf pulled a tiny bronze tool from his pocket. With a twist of his wrist, he sent it coursing through the air toward Ilg. The strange apparatus landed next to Ilg and clamped down on the bridge. Within a few seconds the tool opened into a T-shape large enough for Ilg to grasp. Gulping hot air, Ilg grabbed it with one hand, and clinging to the ramp with the other hand, heaved himself up with all his might.

Standing at last, Ilg swung around and yelled over the volcano's roar, "Wait, Giganta! I will throw a rope!"

Ilg shrugged off his pack and hastily rummaged through the contents. From the bottom of the bag he pulled out a coil of heavy elf twine. Woven by the elf queen's finest weavers, the twine had extraordinary powers if one knew how to use it. Ilg knew of the twine's magic, and the instant he touched it, the cord glowed. He stretched out a length, tied a lasso knot and flung it across to the other side of the bridge in a matter of seconds. "Giganta! Tie this around your waist," he shouted.

Close to the breach in the ramp by then, Giganta dropped to her knees. Hot, volcanic fumes filled the air. Choked with fear she sobbed. "I can't go any further, Ilg!"

"Tie the twine around you, Giganta. It is strong," Ilg shouted. "Don't worry, I won't let you fall!"

"Oh, I can't. I just can't."

"Please, Giganta. You have to. Do it now. *Please.*"

With tears streaming down her face, Giganta picked up the twine. Cold sweat dripped down her back. When she touched the twine, it radiated in her hands. By the time she secured the thin rope around her waist, her whole body glowed. An unexpected strength gushed through her trembling body.

"Now jump!" Ilg commanded.

With Ilg's voice ringing in her ears, Giganta ran to the edge of the bridge. Clinging to the glowing elf twine, she shut her eyes and leaped. Up, up, up she soared. She leaped so high that Ilg lost sight of her. The only thing he could see through the foggy vapors was the glow of the twine as she hurled through the air. Then suddenly, the cord went limp in his hand and wafted down with the end landing at his feet.

"Giganta! Giganta!" Ilg yelled. He called again and again. Frantic, Ilg leaned over the bridge and peered into the lava haze. "Oh, no!" he sobbed. "She's lost. She's lost!"

Just then, as if carried on wings, Gustaf whisked past Ilg and landed near the bronze apparatus. Picking it up, he shoved it into his pocket. "What happened? Where is Giganta?" he asked.

"She's gone," Ilg cried. "I—I don't know—I don't know what happened to her." He handed Gustaf the twine. "She tied the cord just as I asked, but—"

"Alas," Gustaf said and slumped down onto the ramp. Fingering the twine, he examined the end. "Look! The cord, it's been sliced! But how?"

Ilg grabbed the line and studied it. "Yes," he said and searched the bridge. His eyes strained to see through the steaming mist until he could see no more. Above them the air was thick with dark, gnarled clouds; below them Heilaga Hraunvaten roared more ferocious than ever. The volcano had erupted again, and its accelerating red-hot flow caused the bridge to vibrate and crack under the stress. "We must get off the bridge now! Quick, before Brulock falls!"

Ilg and Gustaf ran until their lungs almost burst in the caustic air. Just as they made it to the other side, the top of the bridge collapsed. Hot lava spewed up and over the remnants of the bridge as pumice rock dumped into the lake. Before long over half of the Great Lava Bridge was lost forever in the Great Lava Lake below.

6
Verndari Vakti, Guardian of Brulock

In Icelandic lore it is said elves believe miracles aren't miracles at all. They believe miracles exist as a matter of course. But what happened on this day became known as a truly miraculous miracle throughout the Elf Kingdom. And so it was, for in all of elf history what happened next had never happened before.

✳

"Ilg? Gustaf?"

Shocked to hear Giganta's voice, both the elf and troll swirled around at the same time. "Giganta?" Ilg's voice trembled. "Is that you?" Even though they were surrounded by thick, vaporous fog and could not see, Ilg was sure he had heard Giganta's voice.

"Yes, I'm over here."

Standing on the rocky ledge with their backs to the Heilaga Hraunvaten, Ilg and Gustaf watched in sheer wonder as Giganta's form appeared from the mist as if in slow motion. "Or, I should say, *we're* here," Giganta said. As she came into view, an immense figure nearly three times the size of Giganta loomed behind her.

"Giganta! It *is* you! Thank the queen!" Ilg yelled. But when he tried to go to Giganta, he couldn't. Neither could Gustaf. Their feet were bound to the ground by an unseen force and they could not move. "What? Why can I not move?" Ilg stared at his feet. Around both his and Gustaf's feet glowed a strange, fluorescent green light that felt cool, almost soothing.

"You must stay still," a booming voice thundered from above. "But fear not, no harm will come to you. Soon you will be free." Gustaf and Ilg looked at each other in dismay. Although they could not see the giant's face through the murk, they knew the voice was coming from the massive being behind Giganta.

"Who are you?" Gustaf asked.

"I am Verndari Vakti, Guardian of Brulock, the Great Lava Bridge. I am here to help you. We will rebuild the bridge together but I must warn you once we rebuild the bridge you will have no memory of me. When you return from the Musterihof, the Great Temple, you must cross the bridge again without my help."

"I—I don't understand," Ilg said.

"Ilg, don't worry. Verndari Vakti has great powers," Giganta said. "He has told me he will instruct us on how to reinforce the bridge so it will endure once again."

"Yes. Yes, that's right," Gustaf said. Smiling, he shook one of his feet and in a millisecond lifted his foot straight up. But when he tried to step forward he couldn't move; the other foot was still cemented to the ground by the glowing green power.

"Stand back, elf," Verndari Vakti said, leaning down. "Be advised that you cannot leave now. You must remain and do as I command."

Chagrined, Gustaf set his freed foot down and stood at military attention. "Yes," he said and saluted. "Yes, of course, Verndari Vakti."

Turning his attention to Giganta, the Guardian ordered, "Now, hand Ilg the remaining twine around your waist. It will rejoin with his and then we will begin." As the giant predicted, when Giganta handed Ilg the twine, it knit together with the rest of Ilg's coil so thoroughly in fact that it appeared never to have been severed.

Once the coil joined, the Guardian stretched up to his full height and reached across the rocky path to a lava cliff above the bridge. Using his immense strength he pulled out a large shelf of pumice stone and lifted it high overhead, then brought it down to the edge of the damaged bridge. "Now," he said, holding the rock ledge in place, "use the twine and tie this to the existing bridge so it holds well."

At that moment, Ilg and Gustaf's feet were free again, and without further delay they did as the Guardian commanded. With great efficiency they lashed the stone shelf with the elf twine. They wrapped the twine around and around until the stone attachment held, solid and true. Soon the newly attached part of the bridge glowed with light.

"Good. Hold it steady until I return," the Guardian said and disappeared into the volcanic vapors.

It wasn't long before the Guardian came back carrying a large vessel filled with molten mortar.

Giganta, Ilg and Gustaf, unsure of what was to happen next, huddled together as Ilg held the glowing twine taut. "I cannot think in all of elf history that this has happened before," Gustaf said. "We have never known of such things. Never."

"Nye," Ilg said. "Nor in troll history either. I am sure of it."

"And I have never heard the humans speak of it," Giganta added. "But the Guardian saved me, pure and simple. He is the one who brought me to safety. Otherwise, I would have fallen into the hot lava and perished. Aye, that I would have."

Not another word passed among the trio while they stood stranded at the edge of the bridge waiting for the Verndari Vakti to return. Sweltering from the hot fumes, sweat rolled down their faces as they hunched together in silence. None of them knew what was to happen next.

It wasn't long before the Guardian came back carrying a large vessel filled with molten mortar. With fine-honed precision, he filled all the wide cracks and narrow spaces of the restored arch with the hot matter. When the thick, searing goo was applied, it cooled in an instant, sealing the gaps between the pumice stones and reinforcing the repair. As soon as Ilg and Gustaf had wrapped the twine around each new segment of stone the Guardian adhered it with the hot, liquefied mortar. Working together, they continued to apply this masonry technique until the breach was completely repaired, and the bridge stood strong and looked as it had before.

"Now, you are free," the Guardian said, stepping back into the volcanic mist. Just before the Guardian disappeared, he bellowed, "Giganta, take Ilg and Gustaf to Musterihof and do as I have instructed. Now go."

Calmly, Giganta nodded and took the lead. Without a word the three travelers marched in single file, one by one into the dense haze along a narrow, pebbled trail. Exhausted, unable to digest what had just happened, and ensconced in a thick fog, the three of them wound along a gradual bend. The farther they walked, the more the steaming mist cooled and dissipated. Soon they broke through the swirling murky air to sunny skies and blustery wind.

"Oh, my!" Giganta exclaimed and stopped. Until the fog lifted, she had not known they had been walking along the edge of a steep cliff. Far below, the cold Icelandic sea roared. Ahead was mountainous terrain. "Where are we?" she asked.

"We are here, Milady," Gustaf said. "We are near the Great Temple now, just as we planned. Look! There's the entrance."

Hidden amongst the lava cliff formations was a large, darkened hollow, circular in shape. Sure enough, there it was: the entrance to Musterihof. Formed from rapidly cooling lava over several millennia, the crude, elongated basalt column structure was a sight to behold. Each dark geometric column seemed to meld with the next. Like stacked upright blocks, they formed a thick circular entrance that from a distance resembled a handsome carved sculpture. Giganta marveled at the craftsmanship of the pillars surrounding the gateway. She had never seen anything like it. Touching a column she said, "What fine workmanship. Who did this?"

"We will never know," Gustaf said. "It has always been here—for all eternity."

"Queen Drotti," piped in Ilg, "*maybe* she knows."

"It is doubtful, my friend. For Musterihof, our great temple, has always been here, and our good queen has not." Gustaf took a step forward, and said, "Come. It is time to enter now."

And so Gustaf, Ilg and Giganta walked together into the Great Temple, not knowing what they would find.

✳

Once inside, they came upon a vestibule where a ray of sunlight broke through a large crack in the ceiling; light came through the fracture and lit part of the area. In direct contrast to the rest of the darkened room, the stark shaft illuminated three long stone benches near the travelers. Under their feet, velvety green moss covered the ground and extended halfway up the rocky walls. Heavy dew glistened on lacey spider webs that hung from the rock and moss-covered walls. A slight breeze brushed the dainty webs, making them flutter and sparkle in the semi-darkened space.

"We can rest here," Gustaf said. "We must wait until the inner chamber door opens."

"I'm tired and still hungry," Giganta said sitting down on the far bench. "I would like something to eat."

"Me, too!" Gustaf said. Ilg pulled off his pack and, with a thud, plopped the heavy load on the ground. "Me three," he said and rummaged through the bag. "Here, Giganta, have some bread and cheese." Giganta gratefully took the food and bit into the bread with great relish. "We have rugmol, too, Giganta." Ilg smiled and held up the bottle.

"No. No, thank you. I've had enough of that!" she said.

"Aye," Gustaf said. "A little goes along way, doesn't it? Sabina won't let me have any more of the stuff. She says it's vile. I don't know why she packed it."

"For medicinal purposes, Gustaf," Ilg said, winking at the elf. "A well-known cure."

The three of them munched in silence for a while. Then Giganta spoke. "I have something to tell you, Ilg. Something Verndari Vakti told me. I hope you will understand."

Ilg stopped eating. "The Guardian?" Befuddled, he swallowed his food and looked into Giganta's eyes. "Tell me. I will listen to your words."

Giganta put her food down and reached for Ilg's large hand. Squeezing it she said, "We are related, Ilg—you and I."

"What?"

"Yes, Verndari Vakti wanted me—and you—to know there is love between us. We are distant cousins of the same troll line. It is written that we would meet and important that we know this, for a situation will come later to test us."

"But—I—how—I thought—" Ilg's jaw hung open as he gaped at Giganta. "How can that be?"

"I didn't believe it either at first. But the Guardian knows all of troll history. He not only guards the bridge, but he guards our history too."

"Why, Miss Troll," Gustaf said. "I—does Queen Drotti—does she know of this?"

"Only the guardians of the troll kingdom know," Giganta said. "It is written in the ancient records. The Guardian took me to the Keeper of the Records where I was shown the ledger. That is how I know."

Just then there was a stirring behind them. The moist green moss along the far side of the chamber wall rolled back and a circular stone door appeared where none had been the moment before. The door, made of thick, shiny black obsidian, split open to reveal the Great Temple's inner chamber.

"Behold," Gustaf said, "the Great Temple door opens. We must go in now." Gustaf took off his hat, brushed the crumbs off his coat sleeves and motioned to the trolls to follow. With a great deal of wonder and reverence, the three travelers entered. A balmy breeze enveloped them when they crossed the threshold.

Half a sphere in contour, the dome-like chamber was larger than any building Giganta had ever been in. A stone's throw ahead lay a very large steaming pond, its water the color of a robin's egg. Around the edge of the pond immense black lava boulders were stacked high enough to offer shelter and privacy. The grounds within the inner chamber flourished with tall green grass and a cacophony of wildflowers. Pathways, masterfully set in blue-gray stone, formed intricate geometric patterns around the azure pool. Dotted along the stone walks were carved wooden benches, several clustered around the entrance to the pond. Far above, shining down into the warm water, hung a wondrous orb of crystalline blue. The light emanating from the globe flooded the entire space of the inner chamber. There was no darkness; only filtered beams of blue light pulsated from the great orb and sent soothing warmth into the water.

"Behold," Gustaf said, kneeling. "*Heilaga Fjorn*, our sacred pond. We must bathe ourselves now, before going further. The water will cleanse and rejuvenate us," he said.

One by one, they pulled off their clothing and sank into the luxurious, warm water. The minute they immersed themselves, they felt the waters scrub and clean their bodies. The radiant blue light from the sphere above energized the pool with calming vibrations that relaxed and comforted each of them. There was no sound and none of them spoke. All the woes of their trip melted away. After what seemed a long time Gustaf said, "We can dress now and go further into the Temple, to the sacred chamber. We must see if there is damage. But before we go, we need to taste the sacred water." Gustaf scooped a goblet of water from the pond and passed it to Giganta, then Ilg. Gustaf smiled and smacked his lips after tasting the last of the restorative water. "Now we may go."

Once dressed, Ilg, Gustaf, and Giganta walked in silence along the pathway and into an anti-chamber about the size of the pond itself. Circular in design, the room was filled with huge crystals of all sizes and geometric structures: hexagonal, isometric, tetragonal, monoclinic, and more. The bounteous collection permitted space for only a thin jagged walkway through the crystalline maze. "Come." Gustaf gestured, pointing to a small emerald colored door. "We must go in here." When he touched the door, it slid open.

Crouching down to enter, Ilg and Giganta followed Gustaf into a much smaller chamber. This room was even more spectacular and contained gold nuggets, quartz crystals, amethyst, onyx—semi-precious stones and gems of every kind. In the middle stood a massive obsidian pedestal cut into a tall multi-sided shape and polished to a high gloss. On top was a globe of intense radiance, its light so brilliant it dispelled all darkness. The minute they entered, Giganta and Ilg found themselves unable to move. Their feet seemed riveted to the ground. Only Gustaf walked forward, though he did so with caution.

"Your Greatness," Gustaf said. "We have come as you commanded."

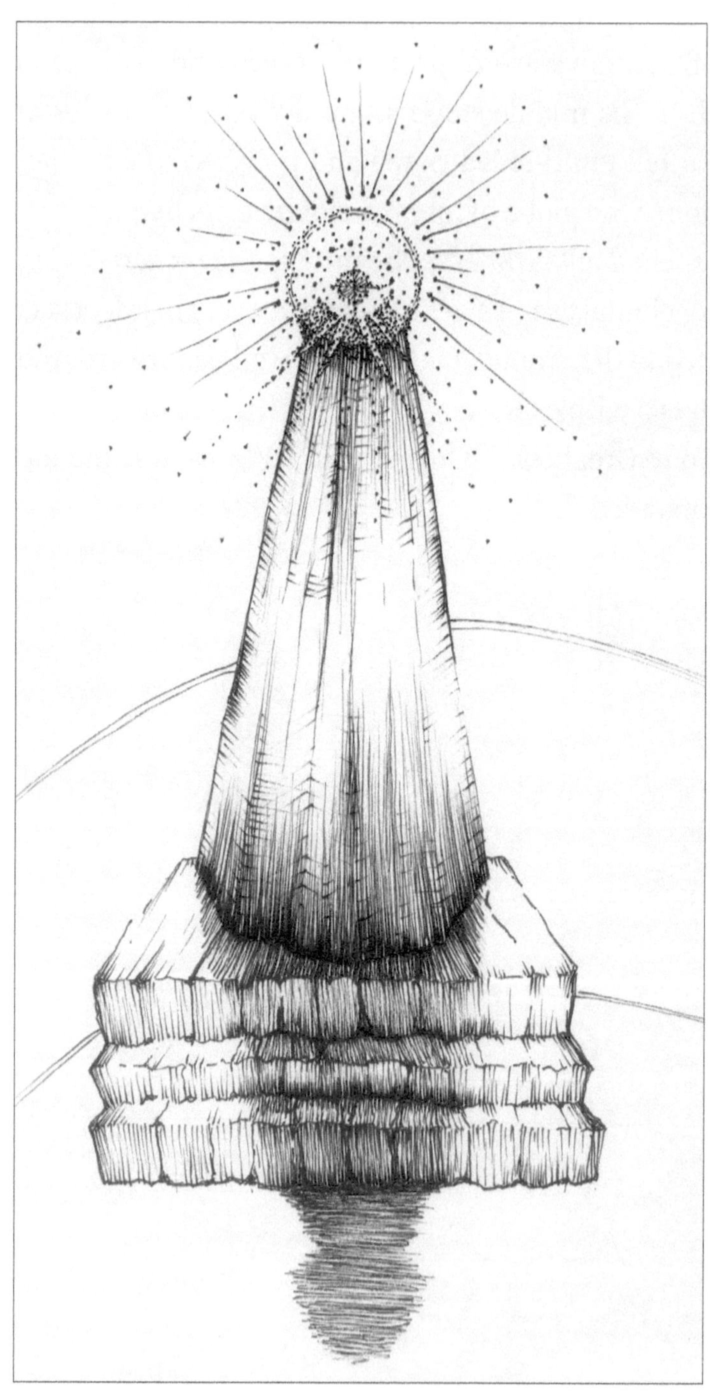

I am Desamlegur Visku, known as the Greatness. Beware.

7

The Warning

The instant Giganta's feet melded with the ground she fell into a deep trance; her body remained motionless as if she was a towering alabaster sculpture. But in the deep recesses of her mind Giganta was awake. Barely breathing, but still alert and cognizant of her inner world, she distinctly heard a loud, clear voice booming inside her head:

I am Desamlegur Visku, known as the Greatness. Beware. A grave and great danger threatens all life in this land. Humankind has perpetrated its will upon all other kingdoms by continuing their underground explorations. This encroachment deep into the land endangers all kingdoms. The human invasion of the ancient volcano's inner channels has disrupted and disturbed the Great Volcano, Eldsplodenryg, causing its molten belly to surge up from the center of the earth's core. This human disturbance will not be tolerated and there will be a reckoning if they do not cease. Eldsplodenryg will fight back and in its vengeance will not only destroy the humans, but almost all other kingdoms and many sacred places. This would mean the end of the land itself. Take this warning back to the humans: If they do not stop, all will be destroyed. There will be no mercy. That is all.

Giganta's eyes popped open the second she was released from her trance-like immobility. Her gigantic body quivered all over. Shaken to the core, she looked at Ilg and Gustaf. "We are doomed," she said with forlorn. "The humans—they are reckless. I must go now to find Inga."

"Of—of course, Milady," Ilg said. Breaking free of the strange temporary paralysis, he surveyed the tiny chamber. "I see no damage here, no cracks or disturbance to the Sacred Chamber. Queen Drotti will be glad of that. We will go now." He glanced over to Gustaf. "Right, Gustaf?"

"Yes. Yes, that's right. Immediately!" Gustaf replied. In a quick about-face, he took the lead and sprinted through the crystalline antechamber, around Heilaga Fjorn and into the vestibule in less than a minute. Both trolls—still tingling from their strange trance—struggled to follow. Huffing from exertion they caught up with Gustaf as he was about to leave Musterihof.

Motioning to both Gustaf and Ilg, Giganta pleaded, "Let us come together for a moment before we leave." And so they huddled together, forming a close ring for what turned out to be the last time the three would see each other for a great long while. When they connected, their combined heart energy formed an almost imperceptible light around them, bonding them together with renewed strength and courage, sanctioning their common resolve for what lay ahead. In this moment, each knew full well the uncertainty of the dire task at hand. The trolls and Gustaf clasped their hands together, and then without a sound nodded to one another and broke from the tiny circle. One by one they walked toward the outer chamber of Musterihof. Just as they were about to exit Giganta glanced down. "Wait!" she cried. "I forgot something!"

With a tremendous sense of urgency, she fled back into the inner chamber, and with Desamlegur Visku's warning still ringing in her ears, raced to the waters of Heilaga Fjorn. There lay her shawl neatly folded on a bench. On top of the shawl in the middle of a long crease was a slender green tourmaline stone about 15 centimeters long. Baffled by the stone's sudden appearance, Giganta whirled around to see who had left it, but she saw no one. Knowing the stone was meant for her, Giganta grasped it and carefully turned it in her hand before slipping it into the safety of her deep skirt pocket.

✳

"Hurry! There's no time to waste!" Giganta shouted as she strode past Ilg and Gustaf who were waiting in the vestibule. Leaving the soothing splendor of Musterihof, she hurried down the narrow treacherous path and began to run. Filled with dread, Giganta ran and ran. When she came to the heavy fog bank, she didn't hesitate, but pushed her way into the thick mist and propelled herself toward the Great Lava Bridge.

"Miss—Miss Troll!" Gustaf yelled after her. "You must wait for *us* to cross Brulock. *You must!*" But Gustaf's words were lost in the swirling mist. Giganta did not hear him, so consumed was she by the urgent need to stop the coming destruction. This was the menace Tarvessa, the Ice Palace, had spoken of—the impending doom she was so afraid would become their fate.

At last Giganta reached Brulock. Gasping for air, her limbs trembling, she stopped to rest for a few minutes at the edge of the Great Lava Bridge. She needed time to think. *She needed Inga's help. How was she going to get to her now?* It would take days to get there from here and by then it might be too late. The humans might have already gone too deep within the earth's crust, further wounding Eldsplodenryg. Then all would be lost—truly lost. Deep in thought, trying to rest her mind, Giganta rubbed the darkly glowing green stone in her pocket. Its smooth surface calmed her.

"Use the stone. Ask Tofraspoti to take you there," a familiar voice commanded. Twirling around Giganta saw the Guardian standing over her. "Verndari Vakti! What do you mean?"

"Tofraspoti is sacred, a special gem having great magical powers that can transport you anywhere instantly, if you command it to do so. That is why it was given to you. It will take you to the humans, but you *must* go now." The words echoed across the Great Lava Bridge and into the fiery molten lake; then Verndari Vakti disappeared in the deep volcanic haze.

"But how?" Giganta said. In a quandary, she dug into her pocket again and clasped the tourmaline between two of her large troll fingers, wondering at its name. "Tofraspoti." Then she heard Ilg's voice.

"Milady," Ilg said as he stepped out of the mist. "We are here now. Gustaf and I will assist. Won't we, Gustaf?"

"Why, yes." Gustaf clambered onto Ilg's shoulder and smiled at Giganta. "Queen Drotti instructed us to be of every help. That she did."

"No," Giganta said. "The Guardian told me I must go alone. This stone, uh—Tofraspoti—" Giganta paused and held up the tourmaline so that Ilg and Gustaf could see it. "It will accompany me." In the dim light the glowing green stone glimmered as she spoke. "Verndari Vakti told me the stone will even take me to Inga if I request it."

"We will follow you then, Milady," Ilg said, "and keep a watchful eye."

Giganta shook her head in dismay. "You must not go to the humans with me; it is too dangerous." She sighed. "Those humans. They'll—they'll not listen if you're there. They know me. I can talk to them. No! I *must* go alone."

"As you wish, Miss Troll. We will wait for you," Gustaf said. "Near the waterfall where we first met."

"Aye," Ilg said. "We'll wait for you and Inga."

And so it was that Giganta readied herself to leave. Teetering at the edge of the Great Lava Lake, she rubbed

Tofraspoti between her two hands until it felt hot. "Take me to Inga's house!" she commanded, and in the next instant she was gone.

✳

Giganta opened her eyes to find herself on the walkway to Inga's farmhouse. The house looked deserted. Cobwebs dripped from the porch steps; layers of dust and grit coated the windows; one windowpane was shattered, and the front door was ajar. When Giganta knocked on it, the door creaked open. Inside, there was no furniture. All the kitchen cupboards were barren, their doors thrown wide open; a few discarded cans rolled across the floor as Giganta entered the room, but that was all. There was nothing else in the cottage. No sound. No sign of her friend, Inga.

Disoriented, Giganta stumbled out of the house. Questions flooded her mind. *What could have happened to Inga? Where did she go? How will I find her now?* She circled the front yard for a few minutes trying to sort out her dilemma and then wandered behind the farmhouse. Giganta stopped short when she recognized the barn standing in the distance. "Inga?" she shouted and rushed toward the immense red barn hoping to find her friend.

She pushed open the double doors. Her tall body cast a long shadow into the barn as she stood for a moment taking in the setting. A mouse skittered across the dirt floor in front of her as she stepped in. The barn was almost empty, all the stalls abandoned. Scattered here and there were remnants of hay bales. At the far end of the cavernous structure a lone sheep was chewing its cud. Startled, the creature looked wide-eyed at Giganta's looming frame, but it did not move. At first unsettled, the sheep looked away, and then resumed eating, nosing nonplussed around what was left of the feed.

"What happened here? Where's Inga?" She spoke as if the sheep understood her meaning.

"Gone," the sheep bleated back.

"Yes, but where?"

"Ask the stone," the sheep said and walked out of the barn into the fallow field below. Her gaze followed the sheep until it disappeared into the mysterious cloudy oblivion that encircled Inga's small farmland.

Taking the sheep's advice, Giganta reached into her pocket and pulled out the green tourmaline. She held the stone up to the diminishing afternoon sun. Spinning the crystal around and around between her two fingers, a glint of pink sparkled from the center of the deep bluish green stone. Curious, she left the barn, and held the stone

Giganta reached into her pocket and pulled out the green tourmaline.

against the fading light, turning it this way and that, until she saw another flash of pink. Then with a slight twist—just the barest movement, a hologram projected itself from the stone and expanded in front of her. There was Inga with two other humans!

Much older and wearier than Giganta remembered, Inga appeared in a darkened enclosure alongside her husband, Roar, and another person whose face she could not see. They were leaning over a desk studying a diagram projected on a bright, well-lit oval screen. For a few moments, they talked back and forth to one another. Then Inga nodded in agreement to both men. She took out a tablet and wrote two words in large letters: *Find Giganta.*

Giganta jerked her head back. Wide-eyed she stared into the hologram again until the pink light abated and the vision melted into Tofraspoti. A strong realization overtook her. *Inga was trying to find her as desperately as she was trying to find Inga.* Giganta grasped the stone and thrust it to her breast. "Find Inga now," she commanded. "Take me to her!"

✳

In an instant, Giganta landed with a thunk in front of a massive cement building that stretched a block long. Only a few cars and trucks were parked in the large, empty gravel parking lot that stretched along the building. Giganta would have recognized Inga's little truck in the fading light even without the weathered sign identifying Inga's sheep ranch.

"There it is," Giganta sighed and strode over to the faded blue pickup. Strewn in the bed of Inga's truck were a pitchfork, shovel, and bucket along with the old familiar metal box where Inga stored her small hand tools. Giganta opened the small chest and peeked inside. Sure enough, there were Inga's tools and a pair of familiar, well-worn work gloves. Remembering the closeness of their friendship, Giganta touched the gloves. "At last," she said. Excited to see her friend again she hurried toward the building.

Her apprehension grew as she approached the heavy metal doors. She had no idea what was in the building, nor did she know where to find Inga once she entered. But with her newfound courage, Giganta spoke aloud, "I *must* find Inga. I must." Buoyed by her mission to deliver Desamlegur Visku's grave warning, Giganta took a deep breath and threw open the enormous doors with one mighty shove.

A lengthy, poorly lit corridor met her as she entered. Closed doors lined the spare hallway on both sides. Unsure of what she might encounter, Giganta knocked on the closest door. When there was no reply she tentatively turned the knob. But it was locked. She tried the next door. Locked too. In fact, every door she tried was locked.

Ahead, a single lightbulb dangled on a thin bare wire from the ceiling, scarcely illuminating the rest of the hall. Giganta turned right when she came to an intersection and walked down another gloomy passageway. In the dim, muted light at the end of the short hall was a solitary door with just a slit of light shining from beneath it.

In big troll strides, Giganta reached the door in no time. She wrenched the doorknob, forcing the door open.

There was a loud crash as it swung back and banged into the wall. A flood of brilliant fluorescent light hit Giganta, temporarily blinding her. She held up her hands to adjust to the glare. That's when she heard Inga's voice.

"Giganta! How—how did you get here?"

"Inga? Is that you? I—I can't see."

"Yes, yes, it's me. I mean it's us! Roar and me, and one other. Come in!"

Giganta stepped into the sterile white room. Fifteen long metal tables lined the area, each covered with active electronic devices. A few blinked and purred, others clattered and beeped. In the room's center an extended island of tables were home to banks of computers and electronic gear. Several big LED flat screens hung from the side walls. Giganta saw one screen had a live video of what looked like lava tubes near the Great Lava Bridge where she had been an hour before. Another screen was monitoring the Great Lava Lake.

"What is this place?" She skirted a few tables trying not to knock over anything.

"A lab. This is where I work. Where we work, Roar and me."

"How long have you been here? I—I went to your house, but you were gone."

"Yes. We had to leave. The government ordered us to evacuate. They want to drill on our land. So we had no other choice but to come here."

Now that her eyes had adjusted, Giganta walked over to Inga. Leaning down, she embraced her friend.

"It is so good to see you, Giganta," Inga whispered. "I've missed you."

"I've missed you too." Giganta looked down with compassion at her friend. "It has been a long time, hasn't it?"

"Too long," Inga said. "Much has happened. The government—it has changed—for the worse, I'm afraid."

"Why are they drilling? What do the humans want now?"

"We are discovering the real reason and it's not good—not at all. You've come at the right time." Inga nodded toward Roar and the other man standing next to him. "We need your help. We meant to look for you but didn't know where to go. You disappeared from town after we moved to the farm. I don't know how, but you heard my call."

"It was Desamlegur Visku—the Greatness—that heard you and sent me here." Giganta lowered her voice. "We are all in grave danger, Inga. All earthly life is endangered because of these humans. I have come to help."

"Tell us what you know, Giganta," Roar said. "We want to stop this madness too."

And so Giganta recited Desamlegur Visku's warning word for word. After she finished, the room was silent except for the clatter and beep of the computers. Finally Inga spoke, "We thought as much. That's why we're here. We've been secretly reprograming some computers."

"I must talk with the humans in charge," Giganta said.

"They won't listen. We've tried," Inga said.

"Then we must *make* them listen."

8
Meeting
Queen Drotti of the Elves

Meanwhile, at the drilling site on Inga's farmland, workman were hard at work. The job foreman motioned to the project engineer who was leaving. He cupped his hands and yelled. "Sir! Stop, sir. Wait!"

Irritated by yet another construction delay, the engineer grabbed the door handle and yanked open the truck door. Without turning he yelled, "Yes. What do you want now?"

"Excuse me, sir," the foreman said, "but the crew reported another drill has broken. This time the bit splintered, broke into a hundred pieces they said. We have to order another one."

"Do it now," the engineer said, whirling to face the foreman. "We can't waste any more time. The Prime Minister will be here in two days to inspect our progress."

"But, sir, we haven't been able to drill for a full week. The bits keep falling apart and now, the workers are afraid. Some of them have left the site."

"Hire more workers, for God's sake! We can't delay."

"But—but word is getting around, sir, that it's—it's the elves. They say the elves are destroying the equipment." The foreman's face turned red. He wheezed and puffed. "A few men have told me their tools have disappeared too. I don't know if I'll be able to hire anyone if this keeps up. Word travels fast, you know."

The engineer threw his cigar down and squashed it with his boot. "Well, try," he said and got into his truck. "Elves," he muttered. "What else?"

✳

From a distance Giganta watched the engineer get into his truck. She had been spying on him for a while. Crouched behind a massive outcrop of lava, Giganta was waiting for him to drive out of the long gravel driveway edging Inga's farm. She intended to ambush him once he left the construction site. She planned to take him to Inga and Roar, who were waiting in a temporary lab where they had assembled more seismic equipment in an old barn not far away.

Meanwhile, the elves were doing a rather splendid job of delaying the drilling. Each day the workers were more and more frightened and were leaving the site. So far, so good, Giganta thought, it was all going well.

Peeping over the lava rocks to get a clearer view, Giganta prepared to lunge at the engineer. In a few minutes she saw his truck coming toward her. As it roared over the dirt road, small lava chips sprayed behind the truck. Surrounded by bleak lava fields the truck wove recklessly along. When it was about 10 meters away Giganta leaped out of her hiding place and onto the road.

Putting both hands up, she bellowed in her deepest troll voice, "Halt!"

The engineer slammed on his brakes. The truck skidded on the loose gravel, stopping a few centimeters from Giganta. But she didn't budge. Fearless, ready to meet any danger, the troll drew herself up to her full height and with hands on her hips scowled at the engineer. Undeterred, the engineer leaned his head out the window and yelled, "Move out of the way!"

"Stop right now!" Giganta roared. The fierce vibration of her voice caused the ground to rumble around them. She grabbed the truck's front grill, hefting it to chest-height and then dropped it so hard the hood popped open. She reached into the engine, pulled a few wires loose and the engine died. Thoroughly intimidated, the engineer got out of the truck and ran toward the construction site, but Giganta was too fast for him. She grabbed him by the collar. "Oh no you don't!" she shouted. "You're coming with me."

The engineer grabbed his chest in terror. "Oh, my God! I'm having a heart attack!"

"Ha!" Giganta laughed. She pulled him upright and tied his hands with the engine wire, then quickly threw an old feed sack over his head. "Not quite, human. You're just scared. You're coming with me!"

"Wh—where are you taking me?" The engineer quaked, his face pale.

"Away from here. Don't worry. I won't kill you even though *you're* killing the earth and everything in it." Giganta glowered at the hooded man.

"My, my men will—"

"Say no more, human." Giganta's voice boomed. "You'll soon see what I mean. Now let's go." Gripping the engineer's collar, she prodded him to move. Still reeling from surprise the engineer tried to resist Giganta's command and dug in his heels. But he was no match for her. Too strong and big for him, Giganta tightened her grip and poked the engineer, urging him along. She half-dragged him as they marched toward the hidden lab where Inga and Roar were waiting.

✳

Gray clouds, packed tight, hung low to the ground as Giganta and the engineer approached the hidden, deserted valley. A merciless wind whipped through their clothing with an angry chill. After they reached the top of the ridge, they trudged down a steep grade and pushed through thick clouds and heavy mist. A fog bank crept from behind, covering their trail as they headed deeper into the valley to Roar and Inga's camp. Within minutes they were hidden in a dank haze. Just as Giganta led the engineer over a massive ledge of rocks, light rain began to fall. Down a tapering path near a broken corral and dilapidated outbuilding, several woolly sheep grazed. They lifted their thick, fleecy heads and watched in silence as Giganta and the engineer slogged by.

By now the engineer was wheezing from exertion. He tried to stop, but Giganta wouldn't allow it. "I'm—I'm worn out," he gasped. "Where are we? I can't see."

Giganta growled. "Come on, engineer! Have you no grit?" she said cutting him no quarter.

Switching to an offensive stance, the engineer barked, "You better let me go. My people will look for me when they find my truck."

"Oh, we've taken care of the truck," Giganta said. "But don't worry, you'll get it back—eventually."

"What do you want with me? What right do you have to kidnap me?"

"Enough. No more talk until we get where we are going." Giganta yanked on the engineer's collar and continued to drag him along the winding trail.

The engineer spat threats and resisted Giganta's tight grip. Not heeding his protests, she pulled him forward until they reached a sheltered part of the valley. From the outside, the faded red barn appeared rundown and deserted. Wall planks were broken or missing. The building's large wooden double doors, hung together by two skimpy metal latches gave the impression the barn had been vacated decades ago.

Giganta led the engineer around to the back of the old building and down a narrow slope. Nudging him further she ushered him down a few stone stairs. "Duck your head," she said and guided him to the outer door of the barn's enormous silo. At the bottom of the stairs, she pulled off the gunnysack. "We're here," she said.

Standing in front of a timeworn wooden door, the engineer shook his head and blinked to adjust his eyes. Bits of straw and debris from his hair fell to the ground. "Phew," he hollered. "What the hell? Where am I?"

"Shush, Giganta," Inga said, peeking around the door. "Keep him quiet. Roar is on the phone," she whispered.

"We've patched into some phone lines and secured it so we won't be traced."

The engineer's eyes grew wide. "What?" he said. "Is that you, Inga?"

"Quiet, human." Giganta grabbed his collar again and led him into the immense grain silo.

At the other end of the vast room stood Roar. With his back to them, Roar waved, signaling the others to be quiet as he continued talking. "Yes. Yes, I understand, but we have Hal—Halvardor—now. Contact the Prime Minister. Tell him we'll meet him half way. Tell him tomorrow and he is to bring no one with him." Roar slammed down the phone and spun around to face the engineer.

"Roar!" the engineer said. "Are you in this too?"

Roar's steely eyes bored into the engineer. "Yes, Hal. Both Inga and I are—and one other."

"Who else is in on this? This is treason, you know. Treason!"

"We are aware of what it is, Hal. You and the Prime Minister think you can fool us but we found out what you're doing, and it's wrong. Criminal!"

"Don't—don't be a fool, Roar. You won't get away with this. None of you!"

"Away with what, Hal? We know what you and the Prime Minister are doing. *You* are the ones trying to "get away" with drilling to the center of the earth. *You* are the ones putting our world in peril. *You're* the one that won't get away with this!"

"We're doing no such thing. The land is fine. Just fine. It's proven out. We've done all the tests."

"We want you to stop drilling," Giganta piped in. "You're killing the land and everything in it! You *must* stop!"

"Hold on, Giganta," Roar said, putting up his hand. "We want Hal with us, not against us. Don't we, Halvardor?"

"I can't see that will happen, Roar. The Prime Minister won't stop and I'm on *his* payroll. He's hired me to engineer this project and I plan to do just that. You won't get away with this. You won't."

"We'll just see about that," Inga said. "Are you ready?"

"For what?" Hal scowled.

"You're coming with us," Inga said. "Untie his hands, Giganta. He will need all the hands he has to get there."

✳

And so Giganta, Inga, and the engineer began their journey to the Elf Kingdom. In minutes they left the old barn and moved further up the valley and across the vast lava field beyond. Wanting to keep an observant eye on the engineer, Giganta took up the rear.

Rain pelted them as they marched over the black, rocky land toward the ridge and waterfall. For what seemed hours they hiked over the jumbled plain, each step harder than the last. On and on they traveled in the coursing rain. Ahead, sheets of water poured down. Rain hit them at a slant and soaked them through and through.

Then, just as they were heading up the ridge to the waterfall, the weather changed; the clouds parted, the rain stopped, and the sun came out.

A familiar figure stood at the top of the ridge, waiting for them. "Giganta!" Ilg bellowed. "Thank Queen Drotti and all that is sacred, you've come back!" He bounded down the rocky surface toward Giganta, but in his excitement he slipped and rolled a few meters.

Laughing, Giganta waved at Ilg. "We're coming," she yelled.

Ilg picked himself up and ran down the ridge to meet them "It is so good to see you again," he said and gave Giganta a big troll hug. "We worried that something might have gone awry."

"So far, it is good." Giganta nodded. "Everything is going as planned." Turning to Inga she said, "Ilg, this is Inga. She is my good human friend. Someone we can trust."

Just then Gustaf, who had followed Ilg, leaped up onto a boulder near Inga and extended his hand to her. "And I'm Gustaf, Head Scout for the Inner Earth Elves. I am most pleased to meet 'cha."

Inga stepped back, amazed. "Oh!" she said. Leaning down, she took his tiny hand and curtsied. "I've never met an elf before—a pleasure."

"And this," Giganta said, raising her voice. "This is Halvardor, the project engineer, the one in charge of drilling."

The engineer, who had been quiet throughout the pleasantries, blustered. "Oh, for God's sake, I can hardly believe you expect me to … to talk to these creatures."

"Indeed," Giganta said and glowered. Her angry stare pierced the air, making the engineer grab his chest as if she'd struck him.

Neither Ilg nor Gustaf spoke but glared at the engineer, each standing erect, ready to protect Giganta and Inga.

"You'll do more than talk to them, Halvardor," hissed Inga. "Much more."

Raising her long arm, Giganta signaled the small group. "Let's go," she said.

Gustaf and Ilg pivoted on their heels and together took the lead, heading up the sharp ridge. Inga grabbed the engineer's coat sleeve and with him in tow, followed them. Giganta held back for a few minutes, scanning the lava plains below for any suspicious activity. Heavy clouds hung low on the rain-soaked land and visibility was poor. Still, Giganta scoured the horizon until she was satisfied that no one followed them. Then she ran up the ridge, closing the gap.

At the crest, Ilg led the bedraggled group to the edge of the plateau where the waterfall crashed down. "We will meet her Majesty Queen Drotti soon," Ilg said. Motioning Giganta and Inga aside, he confided, "We will not be going into the Elf Kingdom this time. It is too dangerous now with the engineer. Queen Drotti ordered the elves to hammer and carve out a small cave ahead and that is where we will meet." Ilg walked over to the engineer. "Follow me. We have to go through a short tunnel. Mind your head."

✳

As chief scout, Gustaf sprinted ahead into the musty, newly forged tunnel. The humans, positioned between Gustaf and the trolls for precautionary measures, entered next. Inga and Hal crouched and scuffled through the rough-hewn opening. The trolls, with their oversized frames were forced to crawl on their hands and knees, squeezing themselves into the cramped tunnel, grunting and groaning as the rough-hewn walls scratched and scraped their arms and torsos. Soon the tunnel widened into a substantial cave. Relieved to be standing again, both Giganta and Ilg dusted themselves off. Stepping aside, they stood back along the far cave wall while Gustaf, Inga, and Hal moved closer to the center of the cavern.

Torchlights flickered, revealing an elevated throne carved out of the stone wall. Off to one side was a diminutive, elaborately embellished arched door. Placed around the cool stone interior were more torches, creating a warm, glowing presence.

Inga and Hal followed Gustaf into the center of the cave, where he stopped. For a moment or two, the room was dead quiet. Then came a rustling, scurrying sound from behind the carved door. The muffled clatter built to a rumble as the small wooden door cracked open. Then came the sound of trumpets blaring as the door opened wide and the chamber filled with noisy banter. Within seconds, the Elf Queen's entourage piled through the doorway and spread into the room. Dressed in full regalia, Queen Drotti's entire court marched around the cave several times while the horns blasted a regal elf tune. The court lined the walls on both sides of the throne and stood in formation. Once they were in position, the horns stopped and there was silence.

An elegant, well-dressed elf stepped forward and announced, "Here enters our revered Queen Drotti!" Again the trumpets blared and the Elf Queen, clad in voluptuous layers of green silk finery, swept in. Nodding to her court as she entered, the queen promenaded once around the cave. She acknowledged the trolls and Gustaf with a gracious smile before taking her place on the throne. "Gustaf," the queen said, "it is so very good to see you again!"

Taking off his hat, Gustaf bowed deeply in reply. "Your Majesty, it is good to be here."

"I see you have brought the humans."

Standing between Inga and the engineer, Gustaf hesitated. With a puzzled expression, he looked back and forth at the human visitors. Then as if a light bulb went off in his head, he pointed at his forehead and nodded. "Ah, of course, Your Majesty!" With a gallant, sweeping motion he said, "May I introduce Giganta's good human friend, Inga."

Bowing her head, Inga curtsied. "Your Majesty, I'm so very delighted to meet you."

Then Gustaf turned to the engineer and scowled. "And this—*this* is Halvardor, the man in charge of drilling to the center of the earth."

Panicked, Hal glanced back at the cave entrance hoping to escape. Red-faced, he clutched his throat, coughing and wheezing. The queen looked Hal up and down in disgust and said to Gustaf, "Bring him closer."

Yanking on the engineer's arm, Gustaf pulled Hal toward the queen. When they came closer to the queen, she thrust her staff out in alarm and said, "That's far enough!"

Queen Drotti stood and with narrowed eyes examined him as if he were tarnished goods. Clearly, he was distasteful to her. "Human, you have threatened our land—your land, and the whole of the earth because of thoughtlessness and greed. This cannot continue." With eyes like daggers, the queen stared at Hal and drummed her fingers on her crystal staff. "What do you have to say for yourself?"

Queen Drotti stood and with narrowed eyes examined him as if he were tarnished goods.

Hal cleared his throat and coughed. When he tried to speak, no sound came out. He turned to Inga. His eyes pleaded with her for support, but she turned her gaze away and did not acknowledge him.

The court murmured and whispered to one another; the queen pounded her staff. "Quiet!" she commanded. "Human, I want to hear from *you*. Only you."

"But I—I can't talk," he whispered hoarsely through dry lips.

"Gustaf, get the human a drink. Something stiff."

From the back of the room, Ilg, who had been watching with great interest, shrugged off his backpack and motioned to Gustaf. He pulled the half empty bottle of rugmol out. "Here, Gustaf. Methinks this will do." In a split second, Gustaf grabbed the bottle and dashed back to the engineer, handing him the flask.

The entire court watched as Hal glugged down a few shots of the potent liquor. "*Ahh,*" the room sighed in unison when the engineer let out a loud burp and re-corked the bottle. Many of the court elves, familiar with the strong, tasty substance, raised a knowing eyebrow. Some turned to each other and licked their lips.

"Hush!" the queen said and pounded her staff. With the barest of smiles she nodded to the engineer. "And now, human, what do you have to say for yourself? Why are you drilling?"

"Heat. Energy," the engineer spit out. "We need geothermal energy to run our machines, heat our homes. Surely, you can understand that."

"Do you not have enough already? I am told every human in your land stays warm and eats well. Why do you want more than you need?"

"Well, er, Your Majesty, uh, it's the government that wants more than it needs. I only work for them. I don't make the decisions."

"What do you mean *you* don't make decisions? You decide when and where to drill. Do you not? Are those not decisions? They are very dangerous ones."

"Well, yes, those are decisions I'm hired to make but the *big* decisions come from the government and I'm not privy to them. The government tells me what to do. That's how it works."

"I see," the queen said. "Then you need to tell your government what damage is being done by their orders to drill."

"With all due respect, Your Majesty, we have done tests to ensure safety. It all checks out. The land is fine."

"Oh? Is that what you and your government think? The land is fine? If that is what you think, you have made a grievous error, human—very grievous. The land is *not* fine."

"I beg to differ with you, Your Majesty. We believe it is."

"Is that so? Well, then we shall see what you think when tested by Eldsplodenryg, the Great Volcano." The queen shot a dark look at Gustaf. "Gustaf, take the human to the edge of Heilaga Hraunvaten so he can see what harm he has caused. Do this now!" And with that the queen rose and left the room, quickly followed by her entourage.

9
Return to Heilaga Hraunvaten

By the time they neared Heilaga Hraunvaten, the Great Lava Lake, the engineer was spent. Exhausted, limp from the rigorous hike and extreme heat, Hal looked down at his boots, which were torn to shreds from the crusty ancient lava fields. He trembled. Sweat rolled down his face. "I can't go on," he said.

"You must," Giganta said. "Mustn't he, Gustaf?"

"Aye, Queen Drotti commands it."

"I'll die if I do," Hal said, rubbing his chest.

"You will not die. We won't let you," Ilg said.

Hal clutched his throat. "I *cannot* go any farther." Just as the last word left his mouth, the engineer toppled over. Gasping on the ground he whispered, "Please."

Ilg leaned down. "The human is ill," he said. "What can we do?"

"The rugmol," said Giganta. "Hand it here. Methinks a little more will help."

Ilg tossed the bottle to Giganta. Uncorking it, she leaned down and gave the engineer a few sips. With his lips wet from the fiery water, Hal nodded with relief but collapsed again on the solid lava bed. He took a few short breaths and gasped. "The air, it's so caustic, so hot. I can't breathe."

"Yes," Giganta said. "Eldsplodenryg is erupting again. Your people have drilled too far into the depths, destroying lava tubes and catacombs. We warned you—Queen Drotti warned you. Now, the Great Volcano is warning you. Open your ears, human, and listen before it is too late."

Breathless, rolling to one side Hal asked, "How much farther?"

"We are near. There's a short tunnel and then we will be at the Great Lava Lake. Come," Giganta said and held out her hand.

Angry, the engineer waved her hand away. Wincing with pain, he rose, first to his knees. Then on one leg and then the other. Heaving his weakened body to a standing position, Hal scanned the terrain. His voice wavered. "I had no idea we'd come this far. My legs are shaking. Are we close?"

"Aye, we are a stone's throw," Ilg said. Positioning himself behind the engineer, Ilg nudged him forward. Gustaf spurted ahead and entered the short lava tube. The trolls, Inga, and Hal trudged along a thin lava trail. Crouching, they followed Gustaf into the tunnel.

Once out of the lava tube, they found themselves near the edge of Heilaga Hraunvaten. The little group huddled together, amazed and shocked at what they saw ahead of them. The molten belly of the volcano had surged, spewing great plumes of hot lava high into the sky. The roar was deafening. Thick black smoke curled above red hot lava that streamed down the volcano into the fiery lake. Soon the searing lava would be perilously close to overflowing and pour over the cliff's edge into the ocean below. Meanwhile, the steam and oppressive volcanic vapors billowed through the mordant air, making visibility difficult.

Gustaf wiped his sweaty brow and turned around to face the group. "We must stop before Brulock," he shouted. "We can go no farther with the humans. Her Majesty's orders."

Turning toward Inga and Hal, Giganta cautioned, "Walking will be dangerous." Hal's pale waxen face worried Giganta. She wondered if he would make it to the bridge. "Ilg," she said, "we must ensure the humans' safety. Stop ahead and let them rest."

"Aye, we can stop over there," Ilg said, pointing to a rocky cliff a short distance ahead. Giganta nodded and struck out across the rocky field with Inga and Gustaf close behind. Ilg took up the rear, positioning himself behind Hal. He sensed the engineer's growing fragility and watched his breathing, prepared to catch the human if he faltered.

Near the rim of the lake, the tiny band stood mesmerized as waves of red-hot lava coursed past them. Paralyzed by what they saw, they watched in disbelief as the torrid mass, built up by pressure, gushed toward the far side of the lake. Before they knew it, the oozing hot lava brimmed over the lake's edge, flowed down to a lower field and over a cliff to the ocean's shore. The molten river of lava sizzled into the salt water causing a massive steam bank that reached up and out into the atmosphere.

"It's catastrophic!" Inga yelled. "See what you've done!"

"Aye," Giganta replied, her eyes wide. Shaking her head, she glared at the engineer. "Eldsplodenryg does not negotiate with those who violate the land."

"How—how do you mean?" Hal nervously laughed. "Y—you think *our d—drilling* did this? Bollocks! That's absurd. Not scientifically possible," he sputtered.

"It seems it is, Hal," Inga said, shaking her fist. "We are doomed if we can't stop this now."

"This is how the Great Volcano responds to greed," Gustaf said. "Watch, human." As if on cue, the earth rumbled and shook, causing the scorching lava flow to spill over the edge toward them. "Quick, we must go over there where it is safer. Hurry or you will perish!" Waving his arm, Gustaf gestured toward a protected alcove built out of crude lava stones. "Follow me," he yelled.

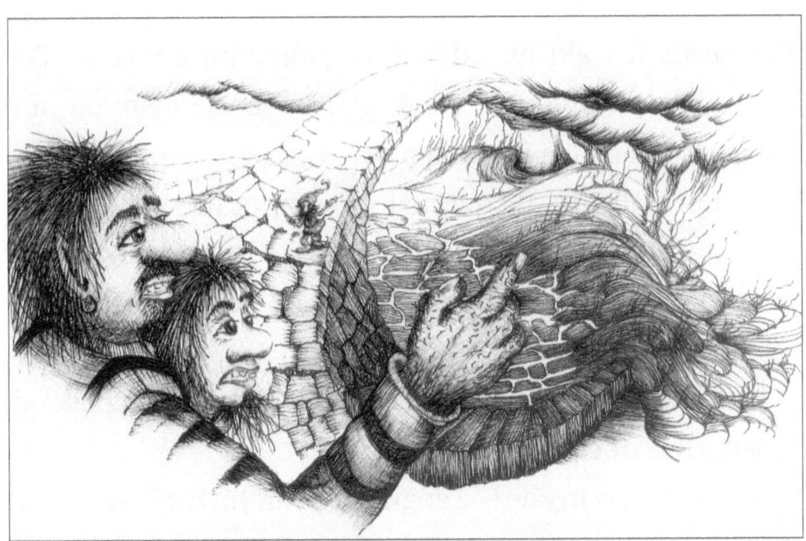

Before they knew it, the oozing hot lava brimmed over the lake's edge, flowed down to a lower field and over a cliff to the ocean's shore.

✳

Gasping for air, the travelers stumbled into the cave-like shelter. Once inside, Gustaf ushered the party to a sunken area where there was an expansive pool of water. He motioned to Inga and the engineer and with great reverence said, "This is a holy place where few have ventured—and never before by humans. Let's rest here. It is cool and safe."

Hal sank onto a narrow ledge. Breathing heavily, he dipped his hand into the cool water. "Ah, at last! My feet could use a good soak," he said and pulled off his tattered boots.

The trolls looked at each other in utter astonishment as they watched Hal splash his skinny, blistered white bare feet in the mineral water. Gustaf shook his head and waved to the trolls to follow him deeper into the cavern, leaving both Hal and Inga at the pool. "Humans are strange creatures," he said. "But we must keep the engineer alive. Her Majesty wishes it and wants his safe return to the drill site. She needs his aid in order to negotiate an amnesty. The queen has commanded me to plant a mechanism on him so we can track his movements."

"A mechanism?" Ilg queried. "I know of no such thing."

Gustaf held up a tiny instrument. "This is new, made from crystals and copper, very small. Her Majesty had it prepared for this exact purpose."

Leaning down to inspect the tracking gizmo, Ilg nodded. "I see. How does it work?"

"I attach this inside the engineer's ear. Its high frequency will beep a secret code to The Queen's Guard and we will know his whereabouts. He will be unaware of the device."

Ilg's eyes grew wide. "Ah," he said. "Do you think the human has seen enough of the destruction?"

"Not yet," Gustaf said and rubbed his chin. "Methinks we must put the fear of Eldsplodenryg into him. But how?" Gustaf patted his stomach. "Oh. My belly roars. I need food. I think better with a full belly, you know."

Ilg plopped down. "There are more rations!" he said and plunged his fist into his knapsack. He pulled out a small loaf of bread.

Gustaf grabbed a chunk of brown bread, took a huge bite and chomped. "Ah, that's better," he said and licked his lips. "Now, where was I?"

"We need to frighten the human," Giganta said.

"Oh, indeed!" Gustaf pointed his finger toward the cave opening. "We'll take the engineer back to Heilaga Hraunvaten's edge and then—" Gustaf fingered his shaggy beard. "Hmm, well, we can't throw him in—but we can scare the dickens out of him! Yes, that's it! First, we, uh, we give the engineer a bit of rugmol and tie him up. Ilg, you will drag him to the bridge and—and leave him." Gustaf stuffed his mouth and dusted off his hands. "I sure could use a drink of rugmol myself. Where is it, Ilg?"

"No! We cannot leave him!" Giganta roared. "And, you cannot touch the rugmol. Don't give it to him, Ilg!"

"Now, lass, we will only leave him for a little while, just enough to scare him. May I *please* have a sip now?" Gustaf held up a measure with two fingers. "Just a little?"

"Nye, you must not, Gustaf. I command it—Queen Drotti commands it!"

"Uh, if you say so. But I don't think—"

Just then they heard a muffled cry near the pool. The trolls and Gustaf glanced at each other and ran back to where they left Hal and Inga. When they arrived at the pool, they found Inga sprawled face down, lying unconscious near the pool. Hal, the engineer was gone.

"Inga!" Giganta gasped. "Inga." Giganta rushed over to her friend, knelt down and shook her. "Inga," she said again and looked to Gustaf. "I fear she's badly hurt. Gustaf, what do we do?"

"Here, Milady, take this." Ilg handed her a small, tin box.

Her hands shook as she pried the lid off. Inside was a thick, powdery pink substance. She looked up. "What do I do, Ilg?"

"Sprinkle a little under her nose. She'll wake up, I promise."

Giganta dusted the powder underneath Inga's nose. In an instant, the woman groaned. "Oh, oh," Inga moaned. "Where am I?"

"What happened, Inga? Where did Hal go?"

Inga blinked and mumbled. "I don't know. We had a disagreement." She massaged her head. "He said he was going back to the drill site to get his men. I told him he couldn't. It was too dangerous and he wouldn't make it. When I bent down to tie my shoe, he hit me with a rock from behind. That's all I remember."

"The engineer," Giganta squinted her eyes and growled under her breath. "We must find him now! You stay here, Inga, and rest. We'll come back for you, I promise." Giganta,

Ilg, and Gustaf hurried out of the shelter and started searching for the engineer.

In a few minutes, Ilg yelled. "Over here!" He picked up a fragment of shoe leather and waved it around. "A bit of his boot sole."

Like a hound dog on a hunt, Gustaf sniffed the ground around the specimen. Soon he picked up the engineer's scent. "This way," he pointed.

Following the engineer's trail brought them harrowingly close to the lake's edge. It wasn't long before Ilg, who was the tallest and had the sharpest vision, spotted the engineer hovering near the Great Lava Bridge. "He's headed to Brulock!" Ilg hollered.

"We have to stop him before he reaches the center. Run!" Gustaf said.

In all elf history no human had ever crossed Brulock and lived to tell. Known throughout the Elf Kingdom there is, at the precise midpoint of the bridge, a hallowed point of entry, a secret doorway that opens into another world— a unique other-dimensional world accessible only to elves and trolls. No human has ever breached this magical portal, though some have tried. But the engineer did not know all this, nor did he understand the danger he was about to confront, and that is why Gustaf, Giganta, and Ilg watched in horror as Hal stepped onto the Great Lava Bridge.

"He won't make it," Giganta sighed.

10
Things are Not What They Seem

Hal dodged flying sparks, leaped over bursts of fire and onto the hazardous bridge. The Great Lava Lake, full to the brink with steaming festering lava, swelled over the far side of the stone ramp. Sweltering in the unbearable heat, Hal flung his jacket into the lava below. Faint, knowing he was trapped, the engineer feverishly pushed forward. Behind, he heard the trolls calling, but he ignored their cries.

"Stop! Stop! You are in grave danger!" Ilg and Giganta waved their arms.

The engineer shrugged off their warnings and kept moving until he reached the middle of the bridge when a mysterious force suddenly clamped his boots to the bridge. Unable to move, Hal stood with his feet stuck to the bridge ramp. Startled by his unexpected immobility, Hal leaned down in horror to find a transparent, green glowing substance winding around his boots. He struggled to move his feet, but they would not budge. Knowing he was in terrible danger, the engineer fell to his knees.

Grabbing his chest, he collapsed. "I can't move. Help!" he cried.

"Indeed you cannot cross, human!" the loud, coarse voice roared from above. "If you try to pursue this endeavor, you will perish."

The engineer did not look up. In the intense heat all he could do was groan.

"Verndari Vakti! " Giganta shouted from behind the engineer. "Stop! We need him. You must not destroy the human!" Rushing up to the engineer, she leaned down to appraise his crumpled body. "He's ill. Can't you see?"

"It is of no consequence. The human cannot pass. It is forbidden!" The Guardian looked down at Giganta and

"Stop! We need him. You must not destroy the human!"

then scowled at the engineer who moaned and writhed, his body half-slumped on the ground. "If the human tries to enter the other worlds, he will die. It is written in the skalds of old."

"*Please*, Guardian. We have to return him safely to the humans. We must," Giganta implored. "Please release him."

Verndari Vakti arose and stretched his enormous body to his full height. With hands on his hips, he howled into the volcanic vapors. A frightful, woeful sound reverberated around the lake, down into the lava flow and out to the ocean's edge. The bridge trembled from the vibration.

Giganta stumbled and fell to her knees. She grabbed the engineer's leg. "Do you want to die, human? You must get up and come back with me or you will."

"No, I don't want to die," the engineer said, his voice weak. "Please help me. I can't move."

Verndari Vakti glared down at the human and said to Giganta, "Be done with it then. Take the human back to his people."

Giganta nodded, stood up and without hesitation yelled, "Ilg! Come! I need your help."

A short distance away, Ilg called to Giganta. "I am here. I will carry the human."

With surprisingly nimble fingers, Giganta untied Hal's boots. Ilg hoisted the human to his shoulders and transported the engineer like a sack of potatoes to safety.

Giganta grabbed the engineer's boots and bowed to the Guardian. "Thank you, Verndari Vakti. Your mercy is most generous. You won't regret it."

"See that the drilling stops—now—for it is nearly too late," thundered Verndari Vakti. "Eldsplodenryg is angry and the other kingdoms are now in peril."

In an instant, the Guardian disappeared into the murky haze.

✳

Once again in the cool, dank cavern, Ilg propped up the engineer so he breathed easier. With sleight of hand, Gustaf quickly inserted the mechanism in Hal's ear.

Meanwhile, Giganta knelt beside Inga. Alert, her friend sat near the pool; her breath had returned to normal. Giganta held Inga's hand. "We will need to rest here until Hal and Inga recover," she said to Gustaf. "Have you a plan yet?"

"Aye," Gustaf said. "A most definite plan, a perfect plan." With a wily smile, he motioned for her to follow him.

"Ilg, stand guard over the humans while I speak with Gustaf."

"Yes, I will watch."

Gustaf steered Giganta deeper into the chamber so their conversation would not be heard. Rounding a stone pillar he held up his hand. "The underground tells me that construction has stopped at the site. The elves have done a splendid job!" Gustaf grinned. "The workers are refusing to work; most have left the job. Methinks the drilling is over—for now. The humans cannot get the equipment to function."

"Good. Good," Giganta nodded. "That will help a great deal. Methinks the engineer is scared. He's seen enough.

Now we have to get him back to his people. Have you a thought on that?"

"Why, yes, Miss Troll." Gustaf winked. "Simple. Now that I have planted the mechanism, I suggest you ask the stone to take him to the waterfall and leave him there." Gustaf nodded. "Yes. Methinks that would be best. There is a deserted road close by. The elves will equip his truck with only enough fuel for him to get back to the drill site. There we will ..."

"Wait, Gustaf," Giganta interrupted, "how will Inga get back? We must make sure she is safe."

"Ah, yes," Gustaf said. "You take Inga and meet Roar and the other human. She will be safe with them.

"Who is the other?"

"You know him—the mayor from your village."

"Viggó?"

"Yes, Viggó. Since you took leave from your cave he's been in touch with Inga and Roar."

"I ... I didn't know. Viggó. He is a good human. I know that."

"Aye, he is working with Roar and Inga in secret." Gustaf raised a finger to his mouth. "Shh. No one must know. No one."

"I understand," Giganta said. "I will take Inga back and then find Viggó to ask for his help. We can work together."

"Yes." Gustaf's face brightened when Giganta pulled out Tofraspoti and warmed the green stone with her hands.

Turning it around and around with her giant fingers she said, "Tofraspoti, take the engineer to the waterfall. Now!"

✳

The next few months sped by so fast that Giganta felt dizzy from all the pandemonium. With Tofraspoti's help, the engineer had been returned to his truck. When he arrived at the drill site, he discovered the area deserted and all construction closed down. Fearful of the elves and their retribution, the foreman and workers had fled, leaving the faulty drilling equipment strewn around the site. Nothing was left except rusty, broken pieces decaying in the damp Icelandic climate.

Meanwhile, unbeknownst to Hal, a secret meeting had been held between the new President of Iceland and Roar, Inga, and Viggó. They had been appointed ambassadors to the Elf Kingdom by Queen Drotti. As commanded by the queen, they negotiated an amnesty that ended all drilling construction.

Giganta joined the meeting but stood quietly in the wings and refrained from speaking. Attentive to the negotiations, she sighed with relief when the meeting ended. At last the land was safe. The ambassadors, jubilant about the treaty, left with the signed agreement.

Giganta and Ilg returned to the elf village and settled there. They were greeted by Queen Drotti and a cheering crowd of elves, and for a while, all was well.

✳

But things are not always what they seem. Not long after the declared amnesty, Hal met with the prime minister in a clandestine meeting on the outskirts of Reykjavik, Iceland's capitol.

"You wanted to see me, Prime Minister?" Hal said.

"Yes. Have a seat." The prime minister peered out the window and then pulled the curtain shut. "This is private," he said and pointed to Hal and then himself. "Only you and me."

"I understand." Hal pulled off his hat and brushed a piece of lint from the brim. "I'm told you've been ousted from office."

"Indeed. Those rascal elves made sure of that! I was shut out of the office. They confiscated all my files. What a mess! I've lost power but I'm not done yet."

Hal nodded. His face turned crimson. "Yes, I'm aware of what the elves are capable of—and let's not forget the trolls." Hal wiped beaded sweat from his brow. "What is this meeting about?"

"I want your help. I need a plan to breach the amnesty and start drilling again." The prime minister pointed to the ground. "There is still a fortune down there. And I want it."

"What do you have in mind?"

"Remember, I never planned to drill for geothermal energy. I always had my sights on 'other things'."

"Yes, of course. We both did." Hal licked his lips. "By my calculations, rare volcanic minerals are still down there. I have all the paperwork and some of the special drill bits hidden." Hal rolled his hat in his hand for a few seconds. "But it's dangerous. I will need to be fully compensated."

"Naturally," the prime minister smirked. "We'll leave nothing out. As you know, these rare minerals are only found here—in Iceland. I've found a market for them. We can make millions!" He laughed and lit a cigar. "But we'll need to start drilling soon."

"Well, with the treaty in place, that will be difficult. I drove by the old site last week. The elves are still guarding the grounds. Besides, there is no useable equipment there. How can we drill?"

"The situation has changed." The prime minister puffed on his cigar and grinned. "A reliable source tells me now that the amnesty treaty has been signed, the elves have moved off and left the site unguarded. We can slip in now. It's time." The prime minister twisted his cigar and studied the smoldering end. "Once we reach the rare crystals, we'll be richer and more powerful than before."

For the fifth night in a row Giganta awoke in the middle of the night. This time, drenched in sweat, a haunting foreboding made her sit up straight in bed. She knew with all certainty that Eldsplodenryg would erupt—and soon.

Hopping out of bed she grabbed her shawl, threw on her slippers, and ran to Ilg's small cottage nearby. "Ilg! Ilg!" she cried. "Wake up!"

Ilg rubbed his eyes and lumbered to the door. When he opened it, Giganta rushed in. "Eldsplodenryg will erupt again, Ilg!" she exclaimed. "We must warn the others now!"

"But—everyone sleeps. Won't it wait for the morning?"

"No! Come, we must ring the warning bell!"

Ilg threw on his heavy shirt and followed Giganta. Together they ran down the avenue toward the square to ring the village bell.

Grasping the thick rope, Ilg pulled on it with all his might.

"Ring it loud, Ilg. Do it now!" Giganta yelled.

Grasping the thick rope, Ilg pulled on it with all his might. The heavy rope was stiff from disuse. As Ilg yanked on the rigid sisal, it softened in his big hands. Soon, the bell rang. Its thunderous clang echoed down all the avenues and into every dark pocket and hallway in the village. Lights flicked on, one by one, throughout the cottages, and all the village elves, still in their nightshirts, sprang into the street, gathering at the village square.

"What is happening, Ilg?" Gustaf shouted from across the square. The sound of the bell was so loud that Ilg barely heard Gustaf's voice. "Ilg!" Gustaf shouted again. "What is wrong?"

"Eldsplodenryg!" Ilg shouted back. "The Great Volcano will blow again. We have to warn everyone!"

At that moment a tremendous jolt and rumbling sound reverberated throughout the tiny elf village. Elves scurried for cover as the earth cracked wide open, piercing the middle of the square.

"Ilg!" Giganta shouted. "Run!"

The ground shook. Ilg stumbled. As the crack grew wider, Ilg lost his footing and slid halfway into the crevice. Desperate, grabbing onto the grassy turf, Ilg tried to pull himself out of the fissure. "Run, Giganta!" he yelled. "Save yourself!"

Giganta ignored Ilg's words and clambered over the shifting earth to help him. "Give me your hand, Ilg," she cried. The earth was rolling now and Giganta, knocked off balance, fell to the ground, unable to reach Ilg. Seconds passed like minutes. Giganta got on her knees and crawled toward Ilg. Reaching the edge of the crevice she thrust out her arm. "Ilg! Hurry, grab my hand now!"

When Ilg clasped her hand, the weight and drag of his body overwhelmed her and pulled her downward. Clenching her jaw, Giganta grit her teeth and dug her feet into the vibrating earth. Tugging and pulling with all her might, she did not let go. Ilg's hulking shoulders rose from the crevice and, with a mighty tug from Giganta, the rest of him emerged from the fractured earth. A minute later, the vent closed and the fierce roaring and rumbling of the earth stopped. Exhausted, both Ilg and Giganta lay limp on the ground.

11
An Arduous Journey

After the earth stopped shaking, Giganta and Ilg stood upright and zigzagged their way through the damaged, jumbled village square to Gustaf's cottage. As soon as they walked in, Sabina served them mugs of much needed hot-spiced tea.

"Me knows this is the engineer's work," Giganta said.

"Aye," Ilg said. "This has the smell of human on it."

For a long moment, Gustaf stroked his long shaggy beard. Then he popped up from the table. "The queen will know what to do. We must go see the queen!"

✳

Queen Drotti swept into the anti-chamber in a huff. Her heavy brocade skirt rustled with fury. She stomped her mighty staff on the stone floor and shouted. "What are the humans doing now? Why are they drilling? They have violated the treaty. They must be found and punished. Gustaf, find out what is happening. Go now!"

"Yes, your majesty. I'll be off!" Gustaf tipped his hat, bowed, and zoomed away.

"Ilg, Giganta, bring the human ambassadors here immediately. This is preposterous. We cannot tolerate this breach."

Giganta bowed. "Your majesty, Inga, Roar and Viggó are working in seclusion at a secret lab. They are doing vital research and might not know of this yet, I fear."

"The Great Volcano opens its bowels and splits the earth apart and the humans do not know of it? Balderdash! We must stop these humans! We must find them!" The queen sat down on her throne with a thud. "Methinks there is treachery here. Much evil and greed."

"Your majesty, we believe Hal and his men are after rare minerals like the crystal on your staff," Giganta said. "They mean to sell these to the highest bidder. We are sure they won't stop until they find what they are looking for."

"They will either halt or Eldsplodenryg will devour them—and us! Go seek out Verndari Vakti. Bring back his counsel." And with that, the queen rose from her throne and stalked out of the room.

✳

Giganta grasped the stone in her pocket and motioned to Ilg to come close. "Tofraspoti, take us to Verndari Vakti," she commanded.

In a blink, the trolls found themselves in front of the guardian's dark lair. Ilg lit a torch and stepped forward. He craned his neck to peek inside for he had never entered Verndari Vakti's domain before. Cautious, Ilg stepped over the threshold of the cave entrance. Once inside, he shone the torch above his head and gestured for Giganta to follow.

Inside the immense cave the air felt warm, almost hot. Thick steam rose from vents on the floor. Great stone pillars reached high into the darkness. The only noise they heard was the shuffling of their feet along the stone floor as they crept into the cavern. At the great hall's center, they halted when a strong magnetic force clenched their feet to the ground. "Who goes there?" roared the Guardian.

"Verndari Vakti, it is Giganta and Ilg. We carry grave news from her majesty, Queen Drotti."

"I know of this news," the guardian said and stepped forward. His immense body shimmered with radiant heat, glistening in the torchlight. "Is the queen safe?" he asked.

"She is well, but angry. The engineer broke the amnesty treaty and is drilling again."

"I could have told her he wouldn't honor a flimsy paper. These humans are wicked and greedy. They will be punished."

"Yes, Verndari Vakti," Giganta said. "Queen Drotti seeks your counsel. She commanded us to return with your advice. Please, Guardian, what say you?"

"Stand fast, trolls, and look upon this." The Guardian reached over his head. He ran his gargantuan fingers along a nearby ledge to a mound of glimmering, golden strands. Grabbing a handful, he leaned down and sprinkled the ground in front of the trolls with thin volcanic glass fiber that looked like angel hair. Each strand glistened in the amber glow as he scattered the delicate threads onto the hall floor. Then a gust of hot air blew the fiber upward and like tufts of airborne seeds, the filament spun around and around. To Ilg and Giganta's surprise, a huge gossamer-like vision stretched across the cave in front of them.

"There," the Guardian said and leaned down to point at the center of the image. "See that? The humans have reconstructed the drill site and they are drilling into the earth right now. This time they are aiming straight to the earth's core. Soon they will hit a river of crystalized rock. There they will meet their end."

The trolls stared, horrified. "Guardian, can we stop them before it's too late?" asked Giganta, trembling.

"You cannot. Greed will be their punishment and their demise."

Without warning, the ground shook under Ilg and Giganta's feet. Small cracks in the dirt appeared around them as the earth vibrated. In the distance they heard a hellacious roar. Then came a violent shudder. Giganta held onto Ilg. When the trolls looked up, Verndari Vakti stared at them with steely eyes. "See. It is happening already," he said. "The humans will regret this forevermore."

"What do we tell the queen, Verndari Vakti?"

"Tell her 'it is done.' That is all. She will know what to do." And then Verndari Vakti disappeared into the depths of the cave.

Ilg and Giganta looked at each other in disbelief. "We must go," Ilg said and gently squeezed Giganta's arm. "Let us walk with caution," he said as he led her out of the cave.

"We need to examine the damage and report everything to Queen Drotti."

✳

And so Ilg and Giganta began their arduous return to the Elf Kingdom. Once they crossed the Great Lava Bridge, the terrain surrounding them changed. Grave signs of destruction greeted them at every turn. Huge volcanic cones shot straight up through the hardened, dense lava. The earth shuddered again and again. For miles, the expansive black fields were dotted with sharp conical shapes and rising steam. What had once been smooth, ancient lava plain was now cracked, ruptured land, making their journey difficult. But they pushed on. Taking the lead, Ilg stopped often to scan the land for dangerous lesions.

Then without warning, they heard a terrifying sound, a roar louder than they'd ever heard. The ground shook violently, rolling and cracking all around them. Vents of hot, blistering steam shot up. The trolls stumbled and fell to their knees. "Ilg!" Giganta yelled.

"We must stop! We can go no further!" Ilg said and thrust his arms up. He rose and steadied himself. "Look." He pointed to a wide, steaming crack. Red-hot lava oozed from the fissure. "Molten lava seeps through here—and over there! We must find another way out."

"But Ilg, there is no other way to go. The volcano has destroyed the land. We cannot go any further. We have to turn back."

"No!" Ilg said. "Giganta, use the stone! Tell it to take us to safety." He helped her stand and lowered his voice. "But not too far, Giganta, we must continue to scout the danger for the Queen."

"Yes. You're right, Ilg." Giganta pulled the tourmaline from her pocket. "Tofraspoti, do as Ilg commands," she said. In an instant, the trolls landed in a cleared, smooth zone away from the worst of the devastation. Upheaval and destruction surrounded them for miles. Shaken by what they saw, the trolls stood speechless.

After a few moments Giganta whispered. "What does Verndari Vakti mean, Ilg, by 'it is done'?"

"I do not know the entirety of his words." Ilg shrugged. "But come. We must go."

Side-by-side, the two friends trudged along in deep despair. Down a steep ravine they hiked, their hearts heavy with grief for the land's future, for all the realms, and most of all for their beloved Elf Kingdom.

When they reached the bottom of the ravine, they heard a loud shout in the distance. "Ahoy there! Ilg! Giganta!"

"It sounds like Gustaf!" Giganta said and hiked up the ravine. Her eyes strained to see their little friend. Cupping her hand around her ear she heard his voice again and spotted a tiny figure scurrying toward them. "Yes! It *is* Gustaf!" she shouted.

Ilg hurried up the ravine and joined Giganta. They stared in wonder as the elf hopped over stumps and stones, across crevices and onto the tops of newly formed boulders. "It *is* Gustaf!" Ilg said and laughed.

"At last I've found you!" Gustaf hopped over to the trolls. "I have great news!"

Giganta and Ilg looked at their little friend, puzzled. "What is this great news, Gustaf? We are so saddened by what has happened. Please tell us!"

"A wonder! A miracle has happened!" Gustaf danced a little elf jig on the flat surface of a large boulder and then yelped, his voice lilting up into the sky. Laughing, he chortled, "Yes, it is another miracle! Who woulda thunk it?"

Kneeling down Giganta looked Gustaf in the eye and pleaded, "Gustaf, please tell us. What is it?"

"They're gone!" Gustaf giggled. His eyes grew wide. "The mountain trolls confirmed it. The engineer and his crew have vanished. Disappeared! All the equipment too."

Giganta gasped. "The mountain trolls? How do they know? What happened? Tell us."

"A wonder! A miracle has happened!" Gustaf danced a little elf jig on the flat surface of a large boulder.

Jumping up and down, Gustaf grinned. His smile was so wide he looked like the Cheshire cat. Twirling around and around and around, all the while bobbing his head up and down, he pranced with glee.

"Please, Gustaf. Tell us!" Giganta shook her hand at the elf and shouted. "Stop, Gustaf!"

Throwing his hands up in the air, Gustaf stopped dancing and stamped his foot. "Ha ha! It's done. They were vaporized!"

Stunned, Giganta and Ilg looked at each other. "This is what Verndari Vakti meant by 'It is done,'" Ilg said.

"Yes!" Gustaf nodded. "The engineer, his men, they drilled too deep. There was an explosion and now they are gone!" He snapped his fingers. "Just like that!"

12
The Gift

It wasn't long before word of the strange occurrence spread throughout all the realms. Once the trolls and Gustaf returned from their journey, Queen Drotti, jubilant the danger had passed, declared a grand celebration. At the opening ceremony the Queen presented Giganta, Ilg, and Gustaf with the highest honor in all the Elf Kingdom: each was given a finely hewn staff made of rare ebony crowned by a deep purple amethyst.

After the opening ceremony, a raucous weeklong party began. The elves and trolls, overjoyed that their kingdom was spared, laughed and danced, ate and drank all day and all night. By the end of the seventh day, the exhausted villagers dropped into their beds, each in a deep slumber—everyone that is, except Giganta.

Weeks before, Inga had urged Giganta to return to the human world. Only after Inga's repeated reassurance that this time she would be treated well did Giganta agree to sneak away for a visit after the Elf Kingdom festivities. Trusting Inga, Giganta walked with her friend to join Roar and Viggó at the waterfall as planned. Together, the four headed toward the small boat harbor near the cave where Giganta had once lived.

When they arrived, Viggó announced to the crowd that gathered, "Now, it is time for us to honor you, Giganta." He held up a long, shiny brass skeleton key and turned to Giganta. "As mayor of this city, I am pleased to offer you, on behalf of all the people living here, the key to your new home." Smiling, Viggó handed Giganta the key. "We have improved your living quarters and made your cave more comfortable in hopes you will be our guest once again."

Giganta showed the key to the crowd. The large group cheered and applauded as she curtsied to them. Then Inga, who was standing beside her, handed Giganta a beautifully wrapped package. "Here, Giganta, this is for you too."

"Why, thank you, Inga. What is in here?"

"Open it." Inga smiled.

Ripping the paper off, Giganta discovered a plain box. When she opened the box, she found yet another package gift-wrapped as elegantly as the one before. "What?" she said, cocking her head toward Inga.

"Keep going," Inga said. "You'll see."

Tearing into the paper, Giganta found another box, inside that was yet another wrapped package. She looked over at her friend again with a curious expression, but Inga just nodded and smiled. From the smallest box, Giganta pulled a gold chain with a golden medallion dangling from it. Set in the medallion's center was a green faceted emerald. Engraved in troll language around the edge of the pendant was a very sacred troll prayer. Giganta caught her breath when she saw the invocation.

"I wrapped the gift in three packages because the mountain trolls instructed me to do so," Inga said. "They said the gift is a high honor, and they wanted you to receive it in the traditional troll way of unwrapping three boxes."

Giganta nodded and inspected the medallion. She knew this gift was a rare sign of troll esteem. She bent so Inga could fasten the necklace around her neck. The crowd roared once again when Giganta stood tall and displayed

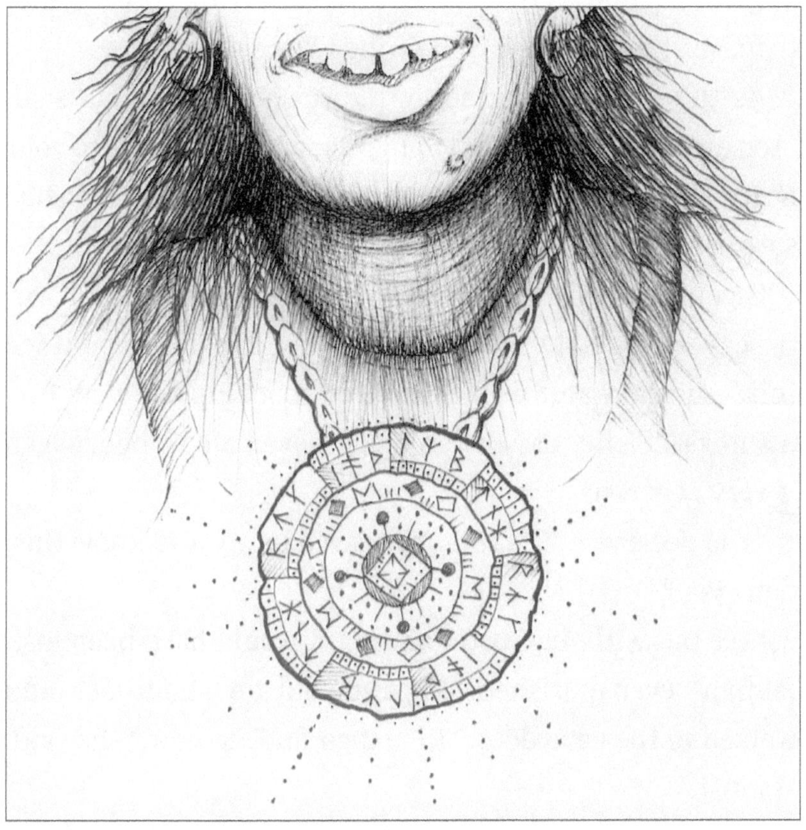

From the smallest box, Giganta pulled a gold chain with a golden medallion dangling from it.

the charmed amulet. "I so wish Ilg was here," she whispered. "He deserves honor too."

"Where is he?" Inga asked. "We expected Ilg to be here as well."

"Gone," Giganta said.

When the crowd dispersed, Inga and Giganta walked over to the cave and talked quietly. "Ilg left after the elf celebration," Giganta said. "He told me he no longer wanted to live in the Elf Kingdom. He said he wanted to be with the other trolls and asked me to go with him." Giganta shook her head. "But I couldn't leave you and the others—not then." Lifting her shawl, she wiped her eyes.

As they entered the newly refurbished cave, Inga said, "You are always connected to Ilg, Giganta. He is close to your heart. He'll come back. I am sure he misses you too. Don't be surprised if he shows up."

Giganta stood in the doorway. Her eyes wandered all over the cave. "It is so beautiful in here now. I wish Ilg could see this," she said and walked around touching the new furnishings. "Plenty of wood, matches, even a new bed. Viggó is very generous."

"You deserve it, Giganta. You saved us all. You know this, don't you?"

"Aye but without Gustaf and Ilg, I would have been lost. Perhaps even perished." Giganta did an about-face and walked to the cave door. "I must go find Ilg now," she said. "I must."

"Of course, but don't forget us and your new home here, Giganta."

Waving farewell to her friend, Giganta pulled out Tofra-spoti and rubbed the tourmaline. "Take me to the waterfall."

✳

Giganta settled amongst the huge boulders in full view of the rushing waters to contemplate her next move. She listened to the roar of the waterfall and gazed toward the town she had just left. Yes, she would miss Inga and Roar—Viggó too, she mused. Even though she felt pleased with her renovated cave, she didn't want to live amongst humans right now. Even so, she wasn't sure why she had rushed pell-mell to the waterfall. *What was she doing? How could she find Ilg here?*

Head propped on her hands, Giganta had to admit it was good to be alone and quiet; there was enough time now to think and reflect about all the strange happenings that had transpired. When she had begun her sojourn, all she wanted was to meet other trolls, to join them, perhaps forever. It was Gustaf who had first helped her, taken her to the Elf Kingdom, and introduced her to Ilg, who tugged at her heart. Now he's joined the other trolls. *Why shouldn't she do the same?*

"Yes," she said, "maybe that's what I will do."

"Do what?" a familiar voice asked.

"Ilg? Is that you?" Giganta swung around, hoping to see him, but no one was there. She slumped down again and waited, for what she didn't know. "What am I waiting for?"

"Yes, what *are* you waiting for?"

"Oh, I don't know—Ilg—something." As if struck by a bolt of lightning, Giganta stood up. "Show yourself Ilg!"

In front of her, a large form came into view. At first, she could just make out the body frame. She couldn't see anything other than an outline. Then little-by-little a body came into sharp focus. When she heard Ilg's hearty laugh, she knew.

"Ilg! It *is* you!"

"Yes, I am here. Come, Milady." Ilg's hand slid through the ethers. "I will take you to the other trolls now," he said. "They are waiting for you."

"But—but—I will miss Inga. Will I be able to return?"

"You are from both worlds now, Giganta. The medallion you received will help you move freely between them. Come. I'll show you how."

Giganta laughed, clasped Ilg's hand and held his fingers in the troll tradition of fondness. Together, they disappeared into the ethers.

Glossary

Brulock: (BREW-loc) The Great Lava Bridge

Desamlegur Visku: (D'SAM (rhymes with Mom)-l'gur (like a growling animal) VISS-koo) The Greatness

Drotti: (DROH-tea) The Elf Queen

Eldsplodenryg: (Elds-PLO-dun-rig) The Great Volcano

Giganta: (GEE-ghan-ta) An adolescent female troll

Heilaga Fjorn: (HI-luh-guh fyorn) The Sacred Pond

Heilaga Hraunvaten: (HI-luh-guh HROHN-vah-ten) The Great Lava Lake

Ilg: (EELga) An adolescent male troll

Jofuvensol: (Joe-FOO-vun-sole) The equinox

Musterihof: (MOOSE-terry-hoff) The Great Temple

Rugmol: (ROOG-mole) Firewater, rye whisky

Tarvessa: (TAR-vess-ah) The Ice Palace

Tofraspoti: (Toe-frah-SPOH-tea)
The magic stone made of green tourmaline

Verndari Vakti: (Vern-DAH-ree, VAHK-tea)
The Guardian of the Great Lava Bridge

Acknowledgements

After returning from a fascinating five-day trip to Iceland, I wanted to write a story about the country. The Icelandic landscape is volcanic, stark, and mystical in nature. All of those qualities resonated with me on a deep level. I was especially intrigued by the cave and troll statue my sister and I discovered on our last morning.

On the long flight home, my mind hummed and soon after my return, I began a short story. Before I completed the first sentence, out popped my protagonist: a female character named Giganta—a troll who lived in a cave in Iceland.

A few months later at a Thanksgiving gathering, I chatted with my friend's grandchild, Stella, who had been a great fan of my children's picture book, *Calvin Splinter & His Splendid Splinter Ideas*. Stella informed me that she "no longer read picture books" and would only read "chapter books." She then went on to explain she wouldn't be interested in my troll story if it were a picture book.

"Okay," I said. "Tell me about chapter books."

"Well, the story is mostly words. There's just one picture in each chapter." She pulled out one of her chapter books. "See," she said and flipped through the pages. Stella grinned and read a few paragraphs to me.

It was then I began to think about middle-grade books and decided to expand my story. Stella's critique was the spark that ignited me to write what is now known as *Giganta, An Epic Tale*. To Stella, I give a special mention and a heartfelt "thank you."

Writing any story that makes it into the publishing arena, be it by traditional or self-published means, is a long and arduous process. There are days of silence, thought-provoking asides, and rude awakenings in the night. If you are a self-published author and illustrator, as I am, it's double-the-work, but not double-the-pleasure. Only the hardy survive. One of the difficulties of a self-published author is finding an audience. This is where public reading forums like open mics and writers' groups come in.

I want to thank all of the folks at the numerous open mics in Friday Harbor and the WhaleTalers, my former writing group, who put on their fifth and sixth grade caps and listened as I read parts of my story in its formative stages. Thank you, thank you!

I'd also like to thank Christy Putney and her two middle-grade humanities classes at Friday Harbor Middle School for participating in my introductory slideshow/lecture about Iceland and listening to me read part of the story. Your attentiveness and astute questions were helpful and encouraging. I remain in your debt.

The San Juan Island community is small, but it is filled with avid readers and writers. I was able to find beta readers for my story without too much trouble. A thank you goes to: Elizabeth Forlenza, Rayleen Hunter, Mariya Masters, and Kat Rose. A special thanks goes to my sister, Libby Cook, who read the first, second and third drafts multiple times and prodded me to keep going even on my darkest days.

To Antoinette Botsford, my editor, friend, and a note-worthy author in her own right: thank you! Your kind suggestions, enthusiasm, and helpful editing make the book a better and more enjoyable read.

And to my special friends: Giganta, Gustaf, Ilg, Queen Drotti of the Elves and all the rest: it's been quite a ride and my sincere pleasure. Thank you from the bottom of my heart.

RA Cook working on another illustration at her drawing table.
Photo by Kat Rose

Author Bio

RA Cook has been a dreamer most of her life. In her early 50s, she enrolled in art school at the Academy of Art University in San Francisco, California to finally fulfill her dream of becoming a skilled artist and illustrator. Little did she know that this step would lead her to write and illustrate stories for children and adults.

As author, illustrator, and book designer, RA Cook published her children's picture book, *Calvin Splinter & His Splendid Splinter Ideas,* in 2018. A magical realism novel, *Going Out the IN Road,* is scheduled to be published in 2022. A sequel will be forthcoming, along with two short story collections, and another Calvin Splinter children's picture book.

Cook works out of her home studio in the San Juan Islands of Washington State. To keep posted and for more information on RA Cook and her work, go to: www.hmapublishing.com.

www.ingramcontent.com/pod-product-compliance
Lightning Source LLC
Chambersburg PA
CBHW020117310726
48970CB00002B/683